gasp

ALSO BY LISA McMANN

THE WAKE TRILOGY
Wake

Fade

Gone

THE VISIONS SERIES
Crash

Bang

Cryer's Cross

Dead to You

FOR YOUNGER READERS
The Unwanteds

Island of Silence

Island of Fire

gasp

VISIONS BOOK THREE

LISA McMANN

SIMON PULSE

NEW YORK   LONDON   TORONTO   SYDNEY   NEW DELHI

SIMON PULSE
An imprint of Simon & Schuster Children's Publishing Division
1230 Avenue of the Americas, New York, NY 10020
First Simon Pulse hardcover edition June 2014
Text copyright © 2014 by Lisa McMann
Cover photographs copyright © 2014 by Thinkstock
Cover photo illustraion by Angela Goddard
For information about special discounts for bulk purchases, please contact
Simon & Schuster Special Sales at 1-866-506-1949 or business@simonandschuster.com.
The Simon & Schuster Speakers Bureau can bring authors to your live event.
For more information or to book an event contact the Simon & Schuster Speakers Bureau
at 1-866-248-3049 or visit our website at www.simonspeakers.com.
Jacket designed by Jessica Handelman
Interior designed by Mike Rosamilia
The text of this book was set in Janson Text.
Manufactured in the United States of America
2 4 6 8 10 9 7 5 3 1
This book has been cataloged by the Library of Congress.
ISBN 978-1-4424-6630-2
ISBN 978-1-4424-6632-6 (eBook)

For the Midwest, with love

gasp

One

It's been a week since the shooting, and we're back on the University of Chicago campus. Ben Galang's eyes light up when he sees us, and he opens his dorm room door wider to let us in. Sawyer and I step inside and stand awkwardly in the crowded space while Trey eases in after us, taking care not to bump his injured arm on the skateboard that hangs from the ceiling next to the doorway.

Ben and Trey exchange greetings, and Trey's face floods with color.

"I didn't know you were coming with them," Ben says to Trey. He sounds genuinely happy to see him.

"Jules talked me into it," Trey says.

Right. Like I *had* to. I try not to laugh. "Yeah, I made

him. He needed to get out of the apartment and get some fresh air. Thanks for getting up early on a Sunday."

"Thanks for saving my life, guys," Ben says.

"Okay," Sawyer butts in, "dude, you gotta stop with that."

"Sawyer is a rather uncomfortable hero," Trey explains.

"Sorry, man—I won't mention it again." Ben grins and points to our seating options.

Trey steps around a pile of laundry to a love seat and carefully picks up a bra from the seat cushion. He glances at Ben, eyebrow raised.

"Roommate's girlfriend spent the night. It's awesome," he says, sounding like it's totally not awesome. He snatches the bra from Trey's hand and tosses it on the bottom bunk bed. "They're slobs. You guys met my roommate—Vernon. He was with me at the hospital. Have a seat. How's the arm?" He perches on the armrest opposite Trey as Sawyer and I sit in the two desk chairs.

Trey shrugs with his good shoulder. "Eh," he says. "It's all right."

Ben presses his lips together but says nothing more.

"So," I say, glancing around the room. Bunk beds, two desks, the love seat, a small TV balancing precariously on milk crates. One desk is fairly neat, and there's a map of the Philippines on the wall above it. "Um," I start again, turning my gaze back to Ben, "you're probably wondering why I wanted to talk to you."

He's wearing different funky glasses, I notice, and I remember that his got broken in the shooting. He smiles. "Kind of. What's up?"

I stare at the carpet, knowing that even though I practiced what I was going to say, this is going to sound so ridiculous. I lift my head and catch Sawyer's eye. He nods, giving me encouragement. My boys are on my side. I'm not alone. But it's still insanity, and I have to be careful. I turn my head toward Ben, who waits, puzzled.

And then I just blurt it out. "Any chance you've started seeing visions recently?"

Two

I expect Ben to laugh, but he doesn't. He studies me a moment. "No," he says slowly.

"Oh," I say. "Um, okay." I peer more closely at him. "You're sure?"

He frowns and looks at Trey. "I'm not sure I understand what's going on here."

"Sorry," Trey mutters. "Yeah, it's a weird question, but she's not insane, I swear."

Sawyer nods in agreement.

"See," Trey continues, "Jules, well, see, it all started . . ." He falters and looks at me.

"A few months ago," I say. "I got this vision of a truck hitting a building and exploding, and I kept seeing it, and it got more and more frequent, interfering with my life, and I kind of felt like I had to do something to, you know, *stop* the thing from happening, or whatever. And it turned out that the building was actually Sawyer's family's restaurant, and the truck was a snowplow with a dead driver—"

"Not like ghost dead—he had a heart attack while driving," Trey adds.

"Right," I say. "We're not *that* nuts. So in the vision the snowplow crashes into Sawyer's family's restaurant, and there's a huge explosion and nine body bags in the snow—"

"Including me in one of those body bags," Sawyer interrupts. "And Jules tried to warn me, but I wouldn't believe her. But she, and Trey, of course," he adds, "ended up stopping the truck from hitting the gas line, so our restaurant didn't explode, but that's how Jules broke her arm . . ."

"And then I thought the whole vision nightmare thing was over and we could just go back to normal, but apparently I, like, *gave* it to Sawyer, and then he—"

"And then I," Sawyer continues, "started seeing a vision too, of . . . of . . ."

The room is suddenly silent and we three glance at each other, and then at Ben, who is looking like a cornered feral cat right about now, wondering if there's a way out of this room, and probably willing to use force if necessary to achieve it.

Trey clears his throat and says quietly, "Then Sawyer started seeing a vision of a mass shooting. At a school."

Ben's eyebrows twitch.

"For the past few weeks," Trey continues, "Sawyer heard eleven gunshots in his head. And reflected in windows, on billboards, on TV screens and other places, he saw the music room on the fourth floor of that building, and he saw . . . bodies. Piles of bodies. And so that's why two high school sophomores were hanging around here last weekend, when the University of Chicago wasn't even officially in session. They weren't checking out the school. They were here to stop a mass murder—or at least keep it from being as horrible as it was in the vision." Trey smiles grimly. "That's why, Ben."

Ben's face is strained. He looks from one of us to the next. "This isn't funny," he says. "It's not funny."

"It's not a joke," I say. "I promise we wouldn't do that to you. I promise."

Ben glances at Trey again, like he trusts him more than us.

Trey nods.

Ben turns to Sawyer and studies him for a moment more. "Piles of bodies?"

Sawyer meets his gaze. "Yes."

Ben stands up and paces in the tiny space. He stops. "Me?" he asks, stabbing his thumb into his chest. "My body?" His voice wavers.

Sawyer drops his gaze to the floor. He doesn't answer.

Three

Trey interrupts the silence. "So you're not having any visions, then?"

At first Ben doesn't appear to hear him, but then, after a moment, he looks at Trey and shakes his head. "What? No. I'm sorry."

Trey leans back and lets out a sigh of relief. "Don't be sorry. This is a good thing."

I catch Sawyer's eye. He looks relieved, but I'm even more stressed, because if it's not Ben, that means we have to keep looking. "Ben," I say, "here's the thing. Just like I passed the vision to Sawyer, I'm worried that Sawyer might have passed the—the curse of the vision on to somebody else." I frown, thinking "curse" sounds too whackjob, but I can't think of a better word. "Like, maybe somebody else who was in that room is now infected, or whatever, and they're seeing a vision of something else—the next tragedy. So . . . um . . . I need to find out. So we can help them."

"*We* need to find out," Sawyer says.

Ben looks at us like we're speaking a foreign language.

"So," I continue, "can you remember everyone who was in the room at the time of the shooting? Do you know them all?"

Ben's face clears slightly, like he's beginning to understand what I'm asking. "I—I know most of them," he murmurs. "Some just by face—it was a combined event with the Motet Choir."

"Can you, like, I don't know—find out everyone's names?" Ugh. I hate this.

Ben bristles. "Okay, this is really getting weird. I'm not sure that's a good idea. I mean, it's pretty strange, what you're asking."

"I know."

"And even the people who haven't left school over it are still pretty shaken up, you know. It's only been a week."

"Totally, totally—so are we," Sawyer says, nodding emphatically. "And, well, if one of them is having a vision of the next disaster waiting to happen, they will definitely stay shaken up, because the visions are—well, they're just horrible, Ben. So yeah, anybody with the vision will stay *very* shaken up, until either they go insane or they die trying to save the next victims." Sawyer adjusts his jacket like he's getting defensive, ready to argue. Just the other night he said he wasn't going to help me with this. Now he's totally invested. I heart that guy.

Ben leans back and sighs. He takes off his glasses and rubs his eyes. "This is so insane."

I give Trey a pleading look.

Trey sits up. "Please," he says, his voice soft and earnest. "We all know how weird this sounds. We just—we don't really have any other choice, you know? We feel like we can't let somebody struggle with this thing alone."

Ben absently starts to clean his glasses with his shirt. "Why don't you call the police or something?"

Trey, Sawyer, and I all wilt. We've been over this before, having vetted this option time and time again. "Because," I begin, but Ben stops me.

"No, it's okay," he says. "I get it. They'd think you're nuts." He frowns as if he's still considering that point himself, and puts his glasses back on.

I close my lips and press them into a defeated half smile, and just look at him, waiting.

Finally he shakes his head. "All right. Fine."

I breathe a sigh of relief as Ben gets up and goes to the clean desk, muttering, "This is so weird," and pulls a few newspaper articles from the desk drawer. He brings them back to us. "We can start here."

Four

From the newspaper articles we glean nine names of students who were actually in the room at the time of the shooting. Ben jots down several more, and then he stops. "This is crazy," he mutters, and looks up. "How do you plan to explain this vision thing to everybody without looking totally nutballs?"

"Very carefully," I say. I actually haven't figured it out yet. "I mean, I know I can't go around asking them all if they're having visions. But I was thinking . . ." I pause as an idea forms. Blindly, I go with it. "I was thinking that maybe we could call a sort of support group meeting for the victims to all get together and talk. And see if anything comes out of it." I glance sideways at Sawyer, who nods.

Ben tilts his head. "That's not a bad idea. We did a

candlelight vigil thing outside the building a few nights ago for the whole campus, and there have been counselors around all week, but maybe I should organize a group with just the victims . . ." He looks at his phone, checking the time. "Actually, tonight would be good, since it's been a week. Kind of like a bad anniversary." He taps his finger to his lips. "I can get contact info for everybody. Can you guys be here at eight?"

"Yeah, no problem," Sawyer says. "The sooner the better."

I glance at Trey. "I think I can get Rowan to switch shifts with me."

"She will. We'll be here," Trey says. He looks at Ben. "I can stay through and help you make phone calls if you like."

Ben smiles. "That would be great." The two hastily look elsewhere, like they're sixth graders crushing on each other, and my heart pinches a bit—could my brother finally have found a nice boy to like?

"Thanks, Ben," I say. "I mean it. You're amazing for . . . well, pretty much everything." I stand up, and Sawyer stands up with me. "I've got to get back if I'm going to take the lunch shift for Rowan. Let us know what's up. We'll see you around eight."

Sawyer and I walk out of Ben's dorm and across the ominous quad that haunted Sawyer's waking hours up until a week ago. Now it only haunts his dreams. I look over the familiar grounds, thinking about last Sunday when we stopped a couple of gun-carrying gay haters from killing eleven people. "I hope they plead guilty," I say in a low voice.

Sawyer nods. "Yeah. I don't exactly want to testify."

My stomach hurts like hell at the thought.

Five things I hate about my life:
1. Apparently there's no end to this insanity
2. The tension at home is probably giving me an ulcer
3. Spring break is over and it pretty much sucked balls
4. I just realized it's my birthday tomorrow. *Tomorrow.* Who forgets important shit like that?
5. It's like things aren't funny anymore

My lunch shift is boring and slow, and Rowan, under slightly heavier surveillance after her little escapade to New York, hangs out in the dining room doing her spring break homework that she wisely waited until the last minute to do. With everything that has happened lately, I'm surprised our parents haven't locked either of us up or gotten suspicious, but they have their own problems, and my dad mumbled something about bad things coming in threes, so I guess with that attitude, he was sort of expecting Rowan's delinquency.

The lull gives me time to fill Rowan in, which makes her even madder than usual that she's missing out on something. I tell her for the millionth time that this isn't something she wants to be in on. She disagrees, and we leave it at that. At five thirty we switch out, and I sneak outside to the alley and find Sawyer waiting for me. We stop for dinner and we're off to UC once again.

We find Ben and Trey in Ben's room a little before eight, Ben at his desk and Trey leaning over Ben's shoulder as he types on his computer.

I knock on the open door and poke my head in. "How many?" I ask.

"We spoke directly to twelve and left messages for the others," Ben says.

"And you didn't forget anyone?"

"I don't think so. Though we didn't bother Tori. She's still in the hospital."

Trey pipes up. "We asked each person we called if they could remember who else was there that night. We're all meeting in the green room in two minutes." He and Ben get up, lock the room, and head in that direction. Sawyer and I follow.

There's a handful of students in the green room already. The guy who was shot in the foot walks in on crutches, and I grab him a chair to put his leg on. A girl sits in a corner of a love seat, clutching her backpack.

Ben's roommate, Vernon, is there, sans braless girlfriend. More people straggle in over the next quiet minutes. "We should have brought refreshments," I say under my breath.

"It's not exactly a party," Sawyer whispers back.

A few people look expectantly at Ben, who glances at his phone and then stands up. "It's been a week," he says with a small smile and a heavy sigh. "And I thought it would be a good idea to just check in with each other, you know?"

A few heads nod.

Ben asks us all to go around the room, introducing ourselves. Trey checks people off his list. I catch his eye and smile, and he smiles back.

Then Ben explains that we don't really have a format; we're just here to talk without any counselors or reporters around to analyze us or judge us or whatever, and I can see people relaxing. I wonder what it's been like here.

Ben looks at the guy with crutches. "Schurman, how's your foot?"

Schurman shakes his head and looks at the floor. "Not great."

"What did your coach say?"

"He's being cool, but obviously I can't play anymore this year. I don't know if, you know, if I'll ever be able to run the same again. I might not be able to play." His voice contains no emotion, like he's become a robot. Like his dreams for the future are over and he's pretending to accept it. I wonder what sport he plays, but I don't ask.

Ben presses his lips together. "I'm sorry, bro."

Schurman shrugs and looks at the floor.

Ben turns to the girl in the love seat. "Sydney? How's it going?"

Sydney's face is strained. "It's going," she says.

"Are your parents . . . handling things?"

"They let me come back here," Sydney says with a shrug. "It's weird. I didn't think . . . you know. That seeing the building, and all that yellow tape . . ."

Someone else nods. "Yeah, I don't ever want to go back in there."

More chime in now, and I sit quietly, watching, feeling the same things they're all feeling, yet somehow I must keep myself distant from those things and stay focused. I know Sawyer is watching too. Looking for signs. Is anybody distracted? Looking out the window, watching a vision play out? It might be too early in the cycle—it's only been a week.

When things quiet, Sawyer says, "I keep having weird nightmares . . . only . . ."

I look at him. So does everybody else.

"Only . . . what?" Trey asks.

"Only, they're not about the shooting. And I'm not . . . actually . . . asleep."

I hear a little shuffling in the room, but I keep my gaze fixed on Sawyer. When no one says anything, Ben says, "You mean like a daydream, only it's scary?"

Sawyer looks at the floor. "I guess. But . . ." He shakes his head. "Never mind. It's not exactly normal. Just . . . trauma, or something."

"What happened to us isn't exactly normal," a girl says. "I guess we can expect weird shit to happen."

I look at her, then back at Sawyer. "What's your . . . daymare . . . about? You said it's not a shooting?" I think I know where he's going with this, and I hope I'm helping.

"No. Something completely different. It's a . . . a truck. Crashing into a building. An explosion," he says. "It's, like . . ." He runs a hand over his eyes. "It's, like, not a dream at all. It's like . . ."

"More like a vision?" Ben asks.

Sawyer laughs weakly. "Well, I'm not—I mean, I wouldn't say that . . . exactly . . . but . . ." He shrugs. "But yeah. I guess that's pretty accurate."

No one chimes in with a similar story. No one appears to be uncomfortable in his silence on the matter. No one flushes or blanches or reacts with their limbs or eyes or anything to indicate they can relate to what Sawyer just described. But they are sympathetic.

Sawyer deserves a Tony Award for that performance. Too bad there's nothing admirable about being a fraud. It's even less admirable when a few of the students hang back at the end of an hour of sharing, giving Sawyer the names of their therapists and urging him to call. Soon.

Five

The truth is, we could all probably use some therapy right now. Hell, we're a mess.

"Well, that was good for everybody, I think," I say later, making myself at home in Ben's room by curling on the foot of Vernon's bed. "I mean, we didn't get what we needed. But at least we've established contact with everybody and they've got our phone numbers."

"Yeah, you can't expect somebody to come forward in front of everybody to say they're seeing visions too," Trey says. He sinks onto the love seat, and Ben sits next to him. Sawyer takes a desk chair.

"How many victims weren't able to come to the meeting, Ben?" I stare at the underside of Ben's mattress. This room smells gross, like a sack of armpits.

Ben takes the list from Trey. "There are three who have left the school completely, one still in the hospital, and one who lives here in this dorm but either couldn't come or didn't want to."

Sawyer looks at me. "How are we going to handle this?"

I think about it. "Start here and work our way out to the ones who left the school, I guess. Who's the guy in this dorm?"

"His name is Clark."

"Should we go up and see him since we're here? I mean, he might have avoided the meeting because he thinks he's losing it." I sit up and slide off the bed.

"I suppose we should," Sawyer says. "But can we just ask him outright? I feel like a big cheat playing things like I just did in the green room."

"Yeah. Let me take this one." I look at Ben. "Will you show us where his room is?"

Ben's already getting up. "Of course."

We knock on Clark's door, but no one answers. Ben hollers down the hallway to some guys toilet-papering the doorway to somebody else's room. "Have you seen Clark?"

They shrug and shake their heads. One holds his finger to his lips to quiet us, and points to the toilet paper.

"Yeah, because no one else will notice what you're doing there if we're quiet," Ben mutters, and I'm kind of digging his sarcasm, which we haven't really seen before today. He looks at us. "I don't know what to tell you. You can hang around and wait if you want."

I look at Trey and Sawyer, and then check the time. "We should go if we want to hit up the hospital tonight, guys."

Sawyer nods. "Yeah. Okay, thanks, Ben. We'll have to come back later this week." He grabs my hand and tugs, but I want to see what Trey does. Watching my big brother have a crush is the only fun I have in my life right now.

Trey smiles at Ben. "Yeah, thanks. I, um, I left my jacket in your room . . ."

I squelch a grin and Sawyer squeezes my hand, probably hoping I'll behave. "We'll go to the hospital and see if Tori is up to having visitors," Sawyer says. "Meet you at the car in thirty minutes? I'm parked on Fifty-Seventh, in front of the bookstore."

Trey waves in acknowledgment.

Sawyer drapes his arm over my shoulders and we walk down to the quad and then out to the street toward the hospital. When we get outside in the dark, he twirls my hair around his finger and smiles at me. "Five bucks says they're making out in Ben's room."

"Dogs, I hope so," I mutter. I lift my chin and we kiss while we're walking, and I feel like even though everything is such a mess, I can actually handle it because Sawyer's here with me.

Six

Tori is awake. It's the first time she's had her eyes open when we've visited her. She doesn't know who we are, but her mom explains and introduces us—we've talked to her a few times before.

Tori's face is unmarred from the shooting. Her dark brown skin is flawless and beautiful. Her hair—a gorgeous mess of tiny black braids—undisturbed. Only her guts were ripped up, and the shreds sewn together. She still has tubes going into her arm—pain meds and antibiotics, her mom says.

My mind flashes to the music room again. The black-and-white checkerboard floor streaked with red. Tori looking dazed, lying against the wall, holding her hand to her stomach as blood poured out between her fingers. . . . Gah. She was the most seriously hurt. I grab the back of a chair as a wave of nausea rides over me. Half the time I feel like I'm still in shock. Like one day, when this is all over, I really will need to be committed.

It feels awkward, us knowing her but her not remembering us. I'm thankful for her mother, who has heard the story no doubt countless times by now from Ben, from us, from others who have visited.

My cell phone vibrates in my jeans pocket, but I ignore it and focus on Tori. "How are you feeling?"

"Terrible," Tori says in a soft voice. "Mostly terrible." She looks at her mom. "Sorry. I'm tired of saying I'm fine."

Tori's mom shrugs and smiles. "Nothing wrong with telling the truth," she says lightly. She turns to us. "It's been very difficult."

"I'm sure it has," I say. "I'm so sorry this happened to you."

"So am I." Her bottom lip trembles the slightest bit. "It sucks."

I reach out and rest my hand on her forearm, and she lets me keep it there. "I'm really sorry. What else is happening? Are you having any nightmares . . . or anything?"

Sawyer leans in. "Jules and I have had some really weird side effects. Just mind tricks, I guess. The psychologist says it's normal."

Tori narrows her eyes at the ceiling. "Nightmares, sure. I think the pain meds are messing with me."

I glance at Sawyer, and I can tell we're wondering the same thing. "Every once in a while Sawyer was seeing a . . . like a vision, I guess. Right?"

"It really helped me to talk about it, though," Sawyer says.

My phone vibrates again in my pocket. Tori doesn't respond.

"So do you want to talk about it or anything?" I ask, trying not to sound odd about it.

"Not really," Tori says. She looks out her window, frowns, and looks away.

Sawyer sits up straight. "Okay, well, is there anything you need? Any homework or stuff from your dorm or whatever?"

She looks at us like the weird strangers we are. "No. My roommate is handling that kind of stuff." She yawns. "And I'm really tired now, so . . ."

Tori's mother stands up on cue. "Thank you both for coming by to visit," she says.

Sawyer and I stand too, somewhat reluctantly. "Sure," I say. I spy a notepad and pen by the bed and ask, "Is it okay if I give you my phone number in case you ever want to talk?"

"Sure," Tori says, but there's no enthusiasm behind it.

I write my name and number on the notepad and sigh inwardly. "Okay. Well. I guess—"

Suddenly there's a flurry of activity outside the room. I turn to look. Trey is running down the hallway toward us like a total lunatic, something he would never do under normal circumstances. I spring to my feet.

"Jules," he calls out in a way that makes my heart clench. He sees me and lunges into the room, face flushed and breath ragged. Tori's eyes widen in fear and Tori's mom rushes over to stand between Trey and her daughter as a nurse comes running in to see what's happening.

"Who are you?" Tori's mom demands.

"What's going on?" the nurse asks.

"He's my brother," I say, grabbing his arm. "Trey, what's wrong?"

"Why don't you ever answer your fucking phone?" Trey shouts, and I feel his breath hit my face. He stares at me, his face breaking. "We have to go."

My stomach twists. "What? What is it? What happened?"

"It's not Dad," he says quietly. "It's . . . it's worse. Come on!"

Seven

"What is it?" I nearly scream as my brother races down the hallway to the elevator. I chase after him.

Trey stops in front of the closed elevator doors and turns so we're standing face-to-face. His dark eyes are pooled with fear and he works his jaw like he does when he's trying not to cry. "It's a fire," he says.

I stare. "What?"

"The restaurant," he says, his voice cracking. "It's on fire."

My throat is closed. I am unable to choke out a single word. I hear Sawyer swear under his breath from somewhere behind me. I didn't hear him approach. I didn't hear anything. And then he's explaining things in gibberish to the interns and security guards who have followed us, apologizing, and then when the people stop crowding around us he's ushering Trey and me into the open elevator and pushing the buttons.

The elevator door closes and my senses return.

"Holy shit," I say. "Oh my God—Rowan?"

"She's fine. She's the one who called me."

"What about Mom and Dad? Tony? Aunt Mary?"

Trey shakes his head, dazed. "I don't know anything else for sure. Rowan was pretty hysterical. She and Tony and Mom were the only ones in the restaurant, and when she called me she was standing outside with Tony. She said she thought Mom got out but now she can't find her. . . ."

"Oh my God, Mom!" I scream.

The elevator door opens to a few curious stares. Sawyer pulls us out of the hospital and points in the direction of the car. We start running, blindly snaking around buildings and down car-lined streets. I pull my phone out of my pocket and see I have three messages. One from Rowan, two from Trey.

"Shit," I say, nearly tripping on a crack in the sidewalk. I dial Rowan, and she answers.

"Rowan! What's happening?"

"Did you find Trey?" She's sobbing.

"Yes, he's with me now. Is Mom okay?"

"I don't know!" Rowan screams. "Just get here!"

"Oh my God," I say as I climb into Sawyer's car. "What about Dad?"

"I don't know! I haven't seen him, and the firefighters won't let me get any closer. Tony's running around to the front and he told me to stay here and watch for them." Her voice hitches in a sob. "Just hurry up!"

"We're driving. Sawyer's going as fast as he can. We'll be there in less than an hour."

"Forty minutes," Sawyer says.

"Forty minutes," I tell Rowan. "Just, whatever you do, stay safe! And call me when you find Mom and Dad."

"I will."

I hang up. "I can't believe this is happening."

From the backseat Trey says, "She told me it was just her and Tony in the kitchen and Mom was out in the dining area. There were only a couple of customers . . ." He trails off. "Tony must have spilled some oil or something."

"Or it could've been a pan on the stove. . . ." Only three of them working. So Dad must have been upstairs. Neither of us says it.

Sawyer grips the wheel and stays silent, concentrating on the road. If we talk, I don't remember any of it. All I need to focus on is that Rowan is okay.

When we get close to home, we can see the lights of police and fire vehicles. The whole block is cordoned off and the sky is filled with smoke, lit up by spectacular, horrible flames. Sawyer parks as close as he can, and Trey and I jump out of the car, pound the pavement, and dodge onlookers, searching for Rowan in the back parking lot.

And she's there, a stranger's blanket draped around her. Trey and I run to her and fold her in our arms and hold her. Her phone shakes in her hand and her face is streaked with tears. "They're okay," she says. "They're on the other side. Dad was on a delivery . . . I didn't know . . ."

"Mom and Dad?" I ask, making sure before the hope can rise too far. "Both of them are okay?"

"Yeah. Tony just called me—Mom twisted her ankle helping customers get out. She crawled out and has been stuck on the other side all this time trying to find me and calling me from other people's cell phones because she left hers in the restaurant. But I wasn't answering because I was trying to call her and you guys and Tony and Dad. Dad was doing the last delivery, which I didn't even know about, and he's back now, and they're both fine." She releases a shuddering sigh. "Tony and Dad are helping Mom walk around the block to meet us here."

"Thank God," Trey says. He hugs us both again. And then we hear warning shouts from firefighters who have been spraying down the buildings on either side of ours—a florist on one side and a bike shop on the other, with apartments above, just like ours. Their buildings are so close to ours that there's no possible way the entire block hasn't gone up in flames, yet there they are, bricks scorched but no sign of interior flames so far. We turn back and stare at our restaurant . . . and our home.

The firefighters' shouts grow louder. They begin to push back from the building, and with a roar and a rush of gasps, the roof falls in on everything we own, everything my parents have worked their entire lives for, everything my father has collected and hoarded for the past ten years. The sparks fly like shooting stars into the night sky.

We stay all night.

Not because we have nowhere else to go. We stay because our parents won't leave, and we won't leave them.

My father's face is like an old worn painting, gray and cracking. He looks eighty years old today as he watches, mourning his business and his precious hoards of recipes and treasures. My mother fusses over us for a while, telling us not to worry. Telling us that we'll get more clothes, of all things—right there in the middle of the parking lot, with her whole life crashing down in front of her, Mom is worried about us being upset that we have nothing to change into. How does one become this person? I don't know.

I don't think my father even notices that Sawyer is there, bringing blankets and food and water and collapsible sports chairs from neighbors and I don't know where else so we can sit down on something other than the cold cement curb of the parking lot. My mother notices, though. When he shows her the chair, she puts her hand on his arm, thanks him with her wet eyes, and sits. He nods and presses his lips together, and I realize how much it means to him to have her approval.

Sawyer hovers nearby. Rowan, Trey, and I all sit together in birth order, thinking about all the things we'll never see again, and every once in a while stating the obvious: "Everything is gone." But it's not everything. It's weird. I have my boyfriend, my siblings, my parents. I'll miss the pillow I pretended was Sawyer. My favorite pajama shirt. My hairbrush and clothes and makeup. But I realize there isn't much else up there that's all mine. Certainly there was no space up there that was all mine. These people—this is what's mine.

I look around, realizing Tony has gone home. "How did it start?" I ask Rowan after a while.

"I don't know," she says.

"But you were in the kitchen, right?"

"Yeah. But it didn't start there, or we might've been able to put it out. Tony and I grabbed fire extinguishers as soon as we heard the smoke alarms, but it was already too late and we had to get out of there."

Weird. I heard my parents warning us about fire hazards in the galley so often that I figured restaurant fires must always start in the kitchen. "I guess they'll investigate."

Rowan shrugs. Nothing is important right now. I look at Trey and he looks at me, and I don't know what to say or do. Nothing is adequate to express how I am feeling. As we turn our eyes back to the smoldering remains of our lives, I hold his arm and rest my head on his shoulder, and we speak at the same time.

He says, "Happy birthday."

And I say, "Did you make out?"

And we look at each other again, absolutely beside ourselves with the strangeness of this all.

"Thanks," I answer. "Best one yet."

"No," he says. "But he touched my face and kissed me."

And that's the thing that makes me start to cry.

Eight

In the morning, Sawyer reluctantly leaves to get ready for school. Neighbors and people from my parents' church come with clothes and food, and we don't know what to do with it all. We put it in the meatball truck and try to figure out where to go from here. There have been offers, but no one is able to put all five of us up together for more than a few nights. I guess hoarders don't tend to have a lot of friends.

Is it wrong that I'm okay with that?

Is it wrong that I don't want to go live in some other person's house?

Now that the fire has been mostly out for hours, the lack of flames helps Dad focus. "We'll go to Vito and Mary's," he says. My uncle Vito and aunt Mary, our hostess, have four kids. The oldest, my cousin Nick, occasionally works—worked—for the restaurant on the pizza holidays. Night before Thanksgiving, New Year's, Super Bowl, prom. Days like those. Nick has three sisters. It's hard to keep track of how old they are, or even which one is which—they're a lot younger and they all look sort of the same. And I'm sorry, but there's not enough room in their house.

"I'll stay with a friend," Trey offers.

"Me too," I say. Yeah, right. I have none.

Rowan frowns. "I'll go with Jules."

"We're all staying with Mary," Dad says, and it's clear that now is not the time to argue. "At least for now."

When it's finally clear to my dad that the firefighters aren't going to let him poke around in the still-burning embers, we pack up the meatball truck and the delivery car and drive away with everything we own. We park in the elementary school parking lot across the street from Aunt Mary's house. We drag our bags of random donations inside and crash in Aunt Mary's living room while her kids are in school.

When I wake up, it's two in the afternoon. I have a crick in my neck and for a minute I can't figure out where I am. But then I hear my mom and dad talking about insurance and it all comes back to me.

Five things that rush through your brain when you wake up midday in a strange place after your house burns down:

1. It feels like somebody died.
2. I wonder what the losers at school are saying about this.
3. I guess that's one way to get rid of all Dad's shit.
4. My hair absolutely reeks.
5. Oh yeah, it's my birthday.

Wait. One more thought:

6. Um, why didn't anyone have a vision to help prevent this?

From the reclining chair I've been sleeping in, I watch my parents talking at the kitchen table. My dad looks like he got hit by a truck. His hair is all messed up and his face is gray leather. I don't think he slept much. Mom looks tired, but not as bad as my dad. She's always been stronger than him. I get up and venture over to them.

Mom looks up and sees me. She smiles and points to a chair. "Did you sleep okay, birthday girl?"

My lips try to smile, but for some stupid reason I'm overcome by the fact that in the midst of this mess, my mother remembers it's my birthday, so I do this weird screwed-up face instead. "Not bad, considering it's a lumpy chair. I just want a shower."

"You've got about an hour before your cousins get home," she says. "Aunt Mary has everything you'll need in the bathroom."

I get up, and she grabs my hand. I stop.

"We had gifts for you," she says through pinched lips.

I swallow hard and feel dumb that I'm so emotional about this. The whole house and restaurant is gone, and I feel sorry for myself because my birthday presents burned up. "I don't need anything," I say. "I wasn't even going to mention it."

"I know." She squeezes my hand. "We'll all go out for dinner—the five of us, I mean. For your birthday."

I glance at my dad, and he nods. He pats his shirt pocket. "I have my delivery tips to pay for it."

It's a joke.

My dad made a joke.

And I remember when I used to love him.

Nine

Sawyer calls when I'm putting on some stranger's donated clothes.

"Happy birthday," he says. "I love you. What do you need most for your birthday?"

"Besides you?"

"Besides me."

"A phone charger."

"That can be arranged. What else?"

I think about this stranger's bra I'm wearing that doesn't quite fit, and cringe. "Some . . . you know. Embarrassing schtuff."

"Ahhm . . . ," he says, and I can tell he has no idea where to begin. He guesses. "Like panty liner shit? And whatever else? 'Cause Kate's got like a whole drawer full of that stuff and she said I could bring you whatever." Kate is Sawyer's college-aged cousin who he moved in with after his dad gave him a black eye.

"Thankfully, no." I think about how much it would suck to have your house burn down on the night before your birthday and also get your period, and I realize things could actually be worse. "Like underwear." I blush. Apparently we haven't gotten to the underwear-discussion stage in our relationship.

"Hey, that's perfect—according to my sources, underwear is the five-week-dating anniversary gift," he says. "Can we go shopping today? Or are you too busy with . . . uh . . ."

"With wearing a stranger's underwear?"

"Yeah." He laughs.

"I can probably sneak out of here for a couple hours. I'll need to be home in time to do my birthday dinner, which should be a wild party." I search through Aunt Mary's bathroom cupboards for a hair dryer. "Can you pick me up in thirty minutes?"

"Aren't your parents around?"

"I don't care. I'm getting out of here for a while, and I'm leaving with you, and it's too bad if they see me. They have enough other stuff to get ridiculous about."

He hesitates. "I don't want to cause them any more stress."

I pause. "No, it's cool. I'll talk to my mom. She's starting to dig you a little."

"She is?"

"Don't tell her I told you."

I can hear the smile in his voice. "Okay, well, if Trey and Rowan need to get out, they can come along. If you want."

I think about it for a moment. I want to be alone with Sawyer, but the bratty cousins will be home soon, and Rowan and Trey need underwear as much as I do. "Yeah," I say reluctantly. "I'll ask them. Even though I just want to be alone with you."

"Me too, baby," he says, and I can hear the longing in his voice. It makes my chest hurt. "But they could probably use a break too."

"Yeah. Make it forty-five minutes." We hang up.

Forty-five minutes later, Mom and Dad are sitting at the table with a woman from the insurance company. Trey and Rowan are ready to go, and my mother seems distractedly relieved to hear we're going shopping for underwear. Sawyer comes to the door with two paper sacks full of stuff from him and Kate, like fingernail clippers and tampons and hairbrushes and razors and crazy hair product and a huge bag of makeup samples from Sephora, which is a store I'd totally shop at if I gave a shit about makeup and had a million dollars. Rowan squeals when she sees it.

My father looks up from the kitchen table, pulled from his thoughts, and his eyes travel from Sawyer's shifting stance to Rowan's delighted expression. Mom watches Dad, but Dad doesn't say anything. He turns his attention back to the insurance woman, and we're home free. "Be back by six," my mom calls after us. "Don't eat any junk."

I almost cry at that. I don't know why, other than it sounds so normal.

We stop at the ATM to get money, thankful all three of us deposited our latest stash of tip money on Saturday, so we didn't lose much. We head to the underwear section of the local everything store. Over the course of thirty minutes, Sawyer transforms from suspicious-looking ladies' department fringe creeper to active participant in camisole and bra fetching. I think it helps that as soon as Trey grabs his boxer briefs and a few other necessities from the men's department, he begins roaming our section, letting everyone know how he feels about the various "design collections." We get some clothes, too, but not very many, because, as Trey points out, we're not really sure if we're going to need our savings for other things . . . like a place to live. Because we definitely don't want to live in Aunt Mary's living room forever.

In electronics we pick up phone chargers for the whole family, which Sawyer insists on paying for. We buy a few snacks to replenish Aunt Mary's cupboards, and then we go. When Sawyer drops us off at five forty-five, Trey and Rowan take the bags inside. And Sawyer and I finally get a few moments of privacy in the car.

Sawyer reaches for my hand. He kisses each knuckle and looks at me with his sweet, sweet eyes, and then he slides his free hand through my hair and leans in, kissing me, our entwined fingers trapped between his chest and mine, our hearts beating through them, and I feel like the fire is inside me now.

After a moment we break apart and I glance nervously at the house windows, but nobody's spying. Sawyer traces my wet lips with his thumb.

"Let me know if you need anything," he says.

"I will."

"You going to school tomorrow?"

"Yeah."

"Good. I felt weird being there without you today."

I nod and look down. "Does everybody know?"

"Yes. It was pretty much the topic of the morning. People are sorry. Mr. Polselli wanted me to tell you he's glad your family is okay."

"That was nice of him." Suddenly I don't want to go to school. It's going to be awkward, not for the first time this year. I glance at the dashboard clock. "I should get inside before my dad starts in with the pregnant bit," I say.

Sawyer smiles. He releases my hand, reaches behind my seat, and pulls out a package with a bow. "Here," he says, handing it to me.

I look at him. "But you paid for the phone chargers and a bunch of other stuff."

He shrugs. "So? You think I want to be known as the guy who got his girlfriend a phone charger and underwear for her birthday? You think I want that hanging over my head the rest of my life?"

The rest of his life.

He catches himself and adds, "I mean, when you're famous and you're out there telling your first-boyfriend stories . . . well, I don't want to be remembered for that."

I laugh, but it sounds hollow in my ears. "I guess I don't want you to be that guy either, since it would only make me look bad when it comes to my choice in boy-friends." I shift my eyes to the package and start opening it, letting the distraction of working the taped corners ease the awkwardness of the moment.

Under the paper is a plain brown rectangular box. "Perfume?" I guess.

"No guessing."

I shake it.

"You might not want to do that."

"A can of soda?"

"Which is somehow better than a phone charger? Open it."

I can't imagine what it is. It's too heavy and big for jewelry, and it's clearly not a book. What else do boys get girls for their birthday?

I open the box and pull out something in bubble wrap. I ease the tape off and unwind it to find: a superhero bobblehead. In my own likeness. And on my cape is a giant letter *I*. I crack up and tap my bobblehead. "Best present ever! How did you do it?"

He looks relieved. "Through a website. I sent them a photo of you."

I examine it. Dark hair, brown eyes, skeptically arched eyebrow. "Yep, that's me." I point to the letter *I* on the cape. "Is that for 'interesting'? 'Intelligent'?"

"No," he says quietly.

"'Important'?" I guess, batting my lashes.

He shakes his head.

"No, wait, I know. 'Insane.'"

"No," he says. "It's for 'invincible.'"

"Invincible," I repeat.

He nods and looks away. "Because I need you to be."

For the first time since the fire, I think long and hard about the vision curse.

Ten

Mom, Dad, Trey, Rowan, and I pile into the delivery car, which no longer has anything to deliver, so I guess it's just a car. We go to one of those Japanese teppanyaki places where the chef does all those spatula and knife tricks and makes an onion volcano and tosses food into his hat and at your face, and we all try really hard to have a good time for the sake of everybody else. It's weird, actually, the five of us all eating dinner together like today is Christmas Day or something. And when I think about how life could be like this for who knows how long, it makes me feel like I'm suffocating.

During a lull in the chef action, Rowan makes a paper airplane with her used napkin and gives it to me for my birthday. Trey presents me with his soup spoon and three mints that he swiped from the register area while we were waiting to be seated. And Mom and Dad slip me twenty bucks, no card or anything—they haven't had time to do more. The chef finds out it's my birthday and does the fake ketchup squirt trick on me—where a red string comes out of the bottle when he squeezes it—and tosses me an extra shrimp, and then after we're done eating, the server brings me a free dessert with a candle in it, which is pretty cool.

When we get back to Aunt Mary's, she and the younger two cousins are frosting a birthday cake for me, so of course I'm forced to eat a piece of that—what a shame. But for once I can't even finish it. My stomach feels like lead. Being here at Aunt Mary's is like a glaring reminder that our home has been destroyed. And finally, as eleven Italians sit around in rare quiet eating cake, Trey asks the question we've all wanted to ask but didn't quite know how.

"So, Pops, what are we going to do now?"

It's startling. My dad looks at him, and at first his face goes to that normal sternness that we've gotten so used to recently, as if Trey was acting up. But then it softens. "We have insurance," Dad says. "We're going to be okay."

"Well, are you going rebuild the restaurant or what?" Rowan asks.

Dad looks at Mom.

"We don't know yet," Mom says. "We're trying to figure that out."

I sit up. "What would you do if you don't rebuild? Do you know how to do anything else?"

Mom laughs and looks offended.

"I didn't mean it like that," I say, even though I think I did. I can't imagine my parents doing anything else. Especially my dad. I'd like to see him get his butt out of bed for a regular job day in and day out.

"And what about our house?" Rowan asks. She glances at Aunt Mary. "I mean, we love you and all, but we can't live here forever."

"We're working on it," my father says. "We'll know more soon. We're trying to figure everything out."

The room erupts into loud conversation about our options, with the cousins giving animated ideas of what my parents could do for a living instead of running a restaurant, such as joining the circus or being professional birthday party clowns. Trey and Rowan get into it, and the house turns back into a typical boisterous family gathering once more. When the doorbell rings, I get up to answer it like I live here.

And it's Ben.

I stare at him, at first confused by how he knew where to find us, but then I gather my senses. "Come in," I say, and a delighted grin spreads across my face. "It's really great to see you."

"Hey," he says. "I'm so sorry. Sawyer called me. I'm—I can't believe it."

"I know." I usher him in. He looks a little frightened by the noise coming from the dining room. "Don't be scared. This is our typical decibel level whenever the family gets together."

"I don't want to intrude."

"You're not. In fact, I think you will lift the spirits of more than just me by your presence." I grin, and he blushes.

I drag him through the breezeway and into the kitchen, which is connected to the dining room, and when Trey notices us, he stops talking midsentence. He shoves his chair back and stands up. His face betrays just how much it means to him to see Ben. Everybody stops talking and turns to look at what Trey is looking at. Ben waves nervously.

"Hi, um," he says, not sure which of the adults to address.

"This is our friend Ben," I say. At the name, Rowan perks up, and I remember she's never met him. I introduce everybody.

"I'm sorry about the fire," Ben says. "You must be, uh, really shocked and sad . . ."

Trey springs to life and comes to Ben's rescue. He

rushes over and turns Ben around and guides him back to the breezeway so they can talk, and Rowan whispers, "He's so cute!"

"I know," I say.

"Why can't you go out with him instead of that other one?" my father booms too loudly, but for once there's no anger in his tired voice.

I stare at him. "Seriously? There are so many things wrong with that question that I don't know where to start," I say.

"What is that supposed to mean? It's just a question."

"He's gay, Dad," Rowan says, licking the frosting off her fork.

"Oh. Well, why didn't you just say that?"

"He's not Italian," Uncle Vito remarks.

"So?" Mom's eyes flash. She turns to me. "Is he—are he and Trey—?"

I shrug. It's not for me to say.

However, there's Rowan. "They made out."

"God, Ro," I say, and I start laughing. "They didn't, actually. Poor Ben."

"Why poor Ben?" Mom says, bristling. "We're good people. What's wrong with us? Is he too good for us?"

"No, he's just scared to death."

"He's not Italian," Uncle Vito says again.

"Exactly, that's why he's scared."

"That's what I'm saying," Uncle Vito says. He picks his teeth. "So what is he, Mexican?"

"Vito!" Aunt Mary and Mom say together.

"What? It's just a question!"

"It's racist," Aunt Mary says.

"Oh, for crying out loud. It is not. People ask me that all the time."

"They do not," Aunt Mary says. "It's too obvious with you."

"Either way, it's rude," Mom says. "He's American like everybody here."

"How do you know?" Uncle Vito asks. Aunt Mary slaps him.

"He's Filipino-American," Trey calls out from the breezeway in an annoyed voice. "So knock it off already. Hey, kids, have another piece of cake, why don't you?"

I grin at Rowan as our younger cousins start shrieking and grabbing more cake and Aunt Mary shoots a look of mock disgust in the direction of the breezeway. It's good to be laughing.

I hear the screen door slam shut and hope it's not Ben running for his life.

And if it is, I hope Trey is running with him.

Eleven

School is weird but we get through the first day, and the second, and the third. People are being nice—for now. But I know how this goes. In a few more days, when their pinprick-size moments of sympathy run out, they'll be talking behind my back again.

After school on Thursday I find Sawyer and we linger outside the meatball truck for a minute while Rowan and Trey climb inside.

"Anything you guys need?" he asks me, like he's asked every day this week.

"Nah. We're good." He's already done enough. "Do you have plans tonight?"

He shifts. "I was thinking about going back to UC to talk to the guy we missed. Clark, I think his name is." He hesitates. "You probably can't come along, right? I mean, I totally understand if—"

"Yeah," I say. "I mean no, I can't. Whoever has the vision curse is going to have to wait." I can't believe I'm saying that, but that's just how it is right now.

"I figured. You don't mind if I just try to keep things moving while you handle your family stuff, do you? I'm just . . . getting a little anxious about it."

I frown at the ground. I want him with me. It's selfish, I know. "Yeah," I say. "Go." I try to sound like I really mean it. Because I should really mean it. Just because my whole life burned up doesn't lessen my responsibility for this vision thing. "I wish we knew how to stop the visions," I say.

Sawyer looks at me. "Do you? Because if we stop it, chances are more people will die."

"Yeah." I scrape the toe of my new used shoe along the asphalt. "I guess I'm just full."

He seems to know what I mean by "full," even though I'm not quite sure myself. Full of shock, full of sadness, full of stress. Too full to deal with the vision. He brushes my hair from my shoulder and caresses my cheek like his hand belongs there. "It's okay. I'll keep searching." He lifts my chin and puts his soft, cool lips on mine.

And then he's gone, and I'm in the food truck with

my siblings, riding to Aunt Mary's. I lean my head against the window as we pass the Jose Cuervo billboard, which looks just as it should.

When we walk into Aunt Mary's breezeway, I can hear the cousins running around, arguing. Trey presses his eyelids shut and shakes his head slowly. Rowan flashes an annoyed look. We have nowhere to hide, and this is getting old. Our home is the living room. I try to be thankful for Aunt Mary and Uncle Vito for opening up their house to us, and for keeping their kids mostly out of the living room so we can feel like we have someplace to call our own, but it's hard.

We venture up the two steps into the main part of the house and around the corner into the kitchen and see a stranger sitting at the table with Mom and Dad. Mom's lips are pressed together so firmly that they're gray, and Dad is staring straight ahead, a vacant look in his eyes. It's frightening.

"What happened?" Trey asks them above the noise of the cousins.

Mom snaps her chin toward us. She looks right through us and shakes her head ever so slightly. Dad doesn't blink.

I stare, and then I grab Trey and Rowan by the elbows and push them toward the living room.

"What the hell," Trey mutters.

"No idea," I say.

"It looked bad," Rowan says.

Later, when we're trying to do our homework, I look out the window and see Dad driving off in the delivery car. Mom comes into the living room, fists clenched like she's going to lose it. She looks at us, and we look at her, and she says, "They believe the fire began upstairs, not in the restaurant."

My eyes widen. Nobody says anything, waiting for Mom to continue.

She does. Her voice is low. "It looks like it started from a worn extension cord in the living room next to some of Dad's . . . stuff."

My heart leaps to my throat.

"With all the hoards of newspapers and books and recipes," she continues, her voice straining, "well . . . there was no chance of saving anything."

I drop my homework and stand up, Trey and Rowan right behind me, and we wrap our arms around our mom. Her tears fall now, and a groan from deep inside her chokes its way out in a coughing sob like I've never heard before. I glance at Trey, and his eyes are as scared as I think mine must be.

Mom cries for a minute, and then she sniffs and wipes her eyes with her sleeve and tries to laugh, embarrassed for losing it in front of us, I guess.

"We're sorry, Mom," Rowan says.

"He feels just terrible." Mom's laugh disappears. She shakes her head. "He walked out in a daze. I don't know where he's going." She lets out a shuddering breath and runs her index fingers under her eyes, absently checking for mascara smudges, and for a split second, in her vulnerability she reminds me of Rowan.

"Do you want me to go find him?" Trey asks.

Mom nods. Her voice cracks when she says, "I don't know what he'll do."

Five things I want to say right now:
1. He's a douche for making you worry.
2. Maybe it would be best if he does just go kill himself, so we can get on with our lives.
3. Okay, those are the only two things I can think of, but dammit, I'm pissed.
4. And now I remember why I don't love him anymore.
5. Because I can't.

Twelve

Rowan stays with Mom, and I go with Trey to find Dad.

"Back home, you think?" Trey asks as he pulls the meatball truck out of the parking lot across from Aunt Mary's. He winces turning the wheel, and I know his shoulder must hurt, even though he doesn't like to admit it.

"Home would be the logical guess," I say. And then I let out a huge sigh. "Now what?"

"I don't know."

"Do you think he's going to . . ."

"No." He puts on his sunglasses when we turn west. "Mom wouldn't send us if she really thought he'd do it."

We drive in silence as the sun sets. Trey pulls into the alley and goes toward the restaurant's back parking lot.

There's a portable fence now around our plot of destruction and there are NO TRESPASSING signs posted. Trey parks next to the delivery car and we get out. He glances in the delivery car's window, probably to make sure Dad didn't blow his brains out in the front seat or something.

The substitute beat cop, Officer Bentley, is doing his rounds. He sees us and comes over. "I'm so sorry about your place," he says.

"Thanks," I reply. "It pretty much sucks."

Officer Bentley turns to Trey. "How's the arm?" he asks. "I heard you took a bullet over at the UC shooting."

I can't quite read the tone of his voice, and maybe it's the uniform, but I think I detect a hint of suspicion. I glance at Trey.

"It's not bad," Trey says lightly, which makes me think he's detecting it too. "I was lucky. It's healing nicely. Starting physical therapy soon." He looks beyond Officer Bentley and changes the subject. "You haven't seen our dad, have you?"

Officer Bentley points his thumb over his shoulder toward the fence. "He's in there." He gives us a grim smile, and he doesn't mention what a coincidence it is that we were hauled into the principal's office a few weeks ago for talking about a shooting at school.

"Thanks," Trey and I say together.

Officer Bentley hesitates, eyeing us, and then he

nods briskly and smiles. "Take care, kids. And stay out of trouble. We've seen your names in the paper more than enough lately."

"Yes, sir," I say. "We'd really like things to calm down too."

He smiles and continues walking.

When he's out of earshot, I mutter, "I was worried he was going to ask a few more questions."

"Me too," Trey says. "We need to stop getting hurt. And be invisible."

"You're telling me."

Trey and I walk over to the opening in the fence and look through it. And there's Dad, on his haunches next to a long, slanted hunk of whatever the roof was made of. Delicately he picks up a nearly unrecognizable scorched book and wipes the ash from it, straining to see in the dying light. And then he sets the book on a pile of other books and pokes through a layer of ash, picking up something else. Something small. He wipes it off and holds it up to the last weak rays of sun, and it glints silver.

"It's the thimble from a Monopoly game," Trey says softly. "Dear God."

Dad slips the thimble into his pocket.

My stomach hurts.

I look at Trey. He looks at me. We drop our eyes and walk away.

. . .

Later, after we've debriefed Mom and everybody else is either in their bed or in a sleeping bag on the floor, I find her again in the dimly lit dining room, sitting at the table holding a cup of hot chocolate, staring out the window into the darkness.

I pull out a chair. She turns at the noise and smiles at me.

"Are you feeling okay, sweetie?" she asks.

"Yeah, I just wanted to see how you're doing."

She puts her warm hand on mine and squeezes. "I'm fine. It's just a house. It's just a business. Replaceable things."

I nod and contemplate that for a long moment. "Waiting up for Dad?"

"Yep," she says, trying to sound upbeat. Trying to sound like the old Mom we're used to.

She takes a sip from her mug and turns back to the window.

After a minute I ask, "Aren't you mad at him? I mean, it's kind of his fault . . ." The words aren't coming out right, so I stop talking.

For a moment I think Mom doesn't hear me. But finally she turns again to smile at me. And then she nods. "Yes, Julia," she says in a measured tone. "I'm very mad. I'm mad that your father won't get help. I'm mad that I can't make him. I'm mad that he can't see . . ." She trails off.

Maybe it's the darkness, maybe it's the circumstances, maybe it's because I'm seventeen now. I'm not sure. But it's the first time she's been so honest with me about her feelings. And I think it's the first time she's treated me like an adult, rather than protecting me because I'm her kid.

"Maybe he'll get help now," I say. But knowing what I know about the Demarco curse, I don't really believe it. He's been in the hospital before for his mental illness, and he won't go near anyone who could put him there again.

I don't think my mom believes it either.

Just then my phone vibrates. I frown and look at it. It's a text message from a number I don't recognize. When I open the message, I almost drop the phone.

It reads: *I want to talk about the vision thing.*

Thirteen

"Are you all right?" my mom asks.

My heart is racing. I look up from my phone. "Yeah," I say. I close the message, slide my phone back into the pocket of my sweatshirt, and yawn. "No big deal. I'm going to bed. Or . . . to sleeping bag, that is." And then I add, "I'm sure Dad will be home soon."

Mom gives my shoulder a squeeze. "Me too."

We say good night. In the living room I hunker down inside my sleeping bag and pull out my phone again.

Sure, let's talk. Who is this? I type in response. It could be anybody. We gave our numbers out freely at the meeting Sunday night.

I wait for a response. It comes: *Tori Hayes.*

My heart races. "It *is* her!" I whisper.

Rowan kicks me and I emerge from my sleeping bag.

"What are you doing under there?" she asks. "Sexting with Sawyer?"

Trey is looking at me too, propped up on his elbow. "Gross," he says. "That's Nick's sleeping bag. You don't know what other body fluids could be in there."

"Yick. Don't be disgusting. I thought you guys were asleep," I say, pushing the sleeping bag off me. My hands are sweating and I'm suddenly nervous about what to say to Tori next. I just need to keep it cool. "One sec," I say, and then I type: *Oh hey Tori. Sorry, didn't have you in my phone. Can Sawyer and I come see you tomorrow after school?*

Tori's response is quick: *I'll be here. Like always.*

I look up and explain in a whisper, "It's Tori. She wants to talk about the visions."

Trey's attitude changes fast. "Oh, wow," he says. "For real?"

"Which one is Tori?" Rowan asks.

"The one still in the hospital," I say. "She got shot in the stomach."

"You were right," Trey muses. "Sawyer passed it on."

I smile grimly. "Looks that way."

Rowan screws up her face. "How's a girl in the hospital supposed to help you figure out the tragedy? She can't even get out of bed."

I shrug. "All she needs to do is tell us what's going on

in her vision. We can figure out the rest. It's not her problem. It's ours."

Rowan and Trey exchange looks, but they don't disagree—this is their problem too. Just because I was the one who apparently took it from Dad doesn't mean we're not all responsible. Me more than them, maybe, because I'm the one who passed it on, but Dad is their dad too. They've got the same crazy genes.

Rowan nods. "I'm helping this time," she says. "Besides, I don't have anything else to do now."

Trey frowns. "I suppose, but you'd better freaking listen to us. This isn't a joke, Ro."

"I know, sheesh. Don't you think I've figured that out after all the times I visit you guys in the hospital?"

"She has a point," I say.

Trey shrugs. "And we could use her since Tori isn't able to help."

We're quiet for a minute as I text Sawyer, letting him know what's up.

"I wonder what her vision is," Trey whispers, just as we hear the breezeway door open and Dad's footsteps in the kitchen.

"Me too," I say. An involuntary shiver races up my spine as I try to force my brain to stop thinking so I can sleep.

That never works, you know.

Fourteen

After school on Friday, as I wait for Sawyer so we can visit Tori, my psych teacher, Mr. Polselli, comes up to my locker. He hands me an envelope.

"This is from the teachers," he says. "For your family." He shrugs and smiles, the laugh lines around his eyes crinkling. He's like the under-the-radar teacher of the year. To me, at least. I don't know why he likes me, but it's been pretty awesome having him on my side. Maybe with all his psychological knowledge he can tell I'm batshit crazy and he feels sorry for me.

"Thanks." I take the envelope and realize it's too dense to be a letter. It's thick. I look up at him as he shoves his hands in his pockets and turns back toward his classroom across the hall.

I slip my thumb under the flap and peek inside. It's money. "Hey!" I say.

He looks back over his shoulder.

"This is money," I say, flustered. We're not charity types.

"Very good," he says with a grin.

"I can't—you don't need to do this." I hold the envelope out.

He stops walking. "Julia, I think you know why you have to take it."

I think hard. Is this a psych question? A life lesson based on book facts? I figure it is. He's that kind of teacher.

"Because it makes *you* guys feel better?" I guess. And I know it's something like that. "You felt helpless to fix the real problem—i.e., make our house and restaurant not burn down—so . . . you do what you are capable of doing to help us and appease your inner . . . whatever?"

"Close enough," Mr. Polselli says. "An A for the day." He slips back into his classroom, leaving me standing there, kind of in shock, when Sawyer finally comes.

We decide that it's best not to have Trey with us when we visit Tori since he acted like a crazed madman the last time Tori and her mom saw us. And they don't know Rowan, so we leave her home as well to help Mom and Dad search for an apartment for us. Sawyer and I make the familiar trek up to Tori's room.

"Hey," I say, lightly knocking on the open door. I poke my head in.

"Come in," Tori says, her voice listless.

Tori's mom frowns when she sees us, like she's not expecting us. I glance at Sawyer.

"We're really sorry about what happened last time we were here, Mrs. Hayes," Sawyer says, looking at Tori's mom. "Trey—Jules's brother—had just run here all the way from campus to let us know that there was a fire at their restaurant."

"Oh dear," Tori's mom says, her face softening immediately. "Is everything all right?"

"It's fine," I say. I don't want them to have to pity us too—they have enough to worry about. "But yeah, I'm sorry for the way Trey came screaming in here, scaring everybody."

"It's understandable," Tori's mom says, and Tori nods.

Sawyer and I pull chairs to the side of the bed, across from Tori's mom. We sit, and I give Tori a reassuring smile. But I'm worried. Will she talk in front of her mom? Does her mom know why we're here? We talk for a minute about how Tori is doing with her slow road to recovery. And then, after we run out of small talk topics, I say, "So, I got your text."

"Yeah," Tori says. She looks uncomfortable, and I don't know what to do. Tori's mom is paging through a magazine.

I mouth the words "Do you want to talk about this now?"

Tori's eyes flit over to her mother and then back to me. She nods. "Yeah," she says. "She knows." It's impossible to read her face. And she's not giving us anything.

"Okay, so if I remember correctly," I say, "we told you about Sawyer seeing a vision as a sort of aftereffect of the shooting. Right?"

Tori nods.

"Are *you* seeing a vision?" Sawyer asks.

"Maybe. I don't know."

"But you're seeing something? Like, a reflection, or on TV, or in the windows?" Sawyer leans forward.

Mrs. Hayes looks up. "The doctor believes it's a side effect of the drugs," she says in a firm voice. "And I agree."

"Mom, please."

Sawyer sits back. "Well, um . . ." He looks at me, scrambling, not knowing what to say.

I don't know what to say either. I wish Tori's mom would go away so we could talk. But we've never seen Tori without her mother here. She never leaves. She even has a cot set up. I take a breath. "Um," I say. "I—I—I think I need to give you some information that is going to sound really weird." I bite my lip and glance at Sawyer.

He shrugs.

"You see," I say, "it really started with me." And I give

her the entire story, even going into the part where Sawyer got his vision, and how we saved people because we prevented the shooting from being worse.

And that's when Tori's mom stops us. She stands up and says, "That's enough."

I swallow hard.

"My daughter has been through a tremendous amount of pain and stress. You are not making her any better with your crazy theories and your—your—making light of the fact that my daughter almost died. This isn't a joke, and if you two really are seeing things, I think you should tell your parents and go to the doctor immediately so you can be treated."

"Mom, I just . . . ," Tori whispers, but then she gives up, like she knows it's futile. She sinks into the pillows and puts her arm over her eyes.

We are motionless, absorbing the words. After a moment, Sawyer stands. He touches my shoulder. "Come on, Jules," he says in a gentle voice. He turns to Tori's mom. "We're really sorry to have bothered you, Mrs. Hayes."

I get to my feet too. "Yes, we're sorry. It was a mistake." I look at Tori. "I apologize if we upset you."

"You didn't. It's fine," Tori says. She lifts her arm. "Mom . . . don't."

Mrs. Hayes ignores the plea and ushers us to the door.

"There's no need for you to visit again," she says, as if she's the decider of what we do.

I mask the panic in my eyes and nod. "All right."

She closes the door behind us and we walk in silence to the elevator and out to Sawyer's car.

"I totally blew it," I say once Sawyer is navigating the streets once more, heading home. "Now what?" I lean back against the seat's headrest.

"I don't know. I'm pissed off. It's not like we forced her to listen to us. She contacted you. And you gave her an opportunity to not talk about it because her mom was there, but she didn't take it."

"How are we going to figure this one out?"

"We're not," Sawyer says. He steps hard on the gas to merge onto the highway.

"But we have to!"

"It's over, Jules. There's nothing we can do. We're not allowed to come back. She's not going to talk to us. Not now. We don't even have a hint of what this one's about."

I scrunch down in my seat and scowl. "I do not accept this."

"Okay," Sawyer says with a wry grin. "But there's still nothing we can do. Your responsibility has ended. We are done."

Funny how I don't feel at all relieved.

Fifteen

I gaze through the car window as we get closer to Melrose Park. And then I text Tori: *Can you at least tell me what happens in your vision? I promise I'll leave you alone.*

She doesn't respond.

Sawyer and I meet up with Trey and Rowan at the library so we can get our homework done in relative peace, even though it's a Friday night. I think we're all tired of hanging out at Aunt Mary's, and besides, I need something to read now that my books are all burned toast. And it's there at the library that I get a response: *I don't know if I can stand this. It's been going on since I woke up after the shooting.*

"Guys, look." I show the message to the others.

"What the heck," Sawyer mutters. "I don't get it."

"It seems obvious," Rowan says. "She can't talk in

front of her mom, so she can only tell you important things via text. Like when her mom is in the bathroom or asleep, probably."

"But why would she make us go all the way over there if she wasn't going to talk anyway?" Sawyer asks.

"I don't know," Rowan says. "Maybe she's sneaky, and she thought she'd be able to get rid of her mom for a little bit, but it didn't work."

"Spoken like a pro," Trey remarks.

Rowan sticks out her tongue at him.

Sawyer tilts his head, thinking. "Yeah, maybe Rowan is right. Tori realized she doesn't have the support she thought she had from her mom, and now can only text when her mom isn't around. It wouldn't surprise me if Mrs. Hayes looks over Tori's shoulder and reads every text she sends." He pauses. "I mean, don't get me wrong. It's great Mrs. Hayes has dropped everything to be at her daughter's side. It just seems like she's gone a little overboard."

"So what should I reply?" I ask. "Just tell her we can stop the visions but only if she tells us everything?" I shake my head, trying to imagine getting all the info we need from her text messages.

"Yeah," Trey says. "Don't waste time asking her what's up with her mother. Just get right to the point."

I type: *We can help but we need to know everything about your vision so we can stop the tragedy from happening. It's a tragedy of some sort, isn't it?* I look up, my finger hovering over the send button. "Okay?"

Everybody nods. I press the button.

Yes, comes the reply.

Sawyer groans. "Come on, Tori. Give us something."

"Hold on, she's typing more," I say.

We stare, breathless, waiting to find out what our next impossible mission will be.

"I think I'm going to throw up," Sawyer whispers.

"Me too," I say.

And finally: *Must hurry—there's a house. Sirens. Ambulance. Paramedics taking bodies out on stretchers.*

I read the text aloud, and then type: *Do you see any street signs? What kind of house? Is there a house number? How many bodies? Can you tell what's wrong with them?* I look around the group. "Okay?"

They nod. I send. And we wait.

She doesn't reply.

After a few moments of silence, all of us willing my phone to vibrate, willing Tori's name to show up on my screen, we give up and try to do our homework for a while.

"This is agonizing," Rowan says as the "Library closes in ten minutes" recording breaks our concentration. We pack up and make our way through the teen section, each of us grabbing a few books to borrow, and stop at the checkout desk.

Once outside, I look at my phone again to make sure I didn't miss anything. I echo Rowan's words. "It *is* agonizing. It must be for Tori, too. Especially since it seems like she thought it was okay to talk about this in front of her mom." I think back to my vision—how horrible and alone I felt. And that helps strengthen my weakened resolve to help Tori.

I say a quick good night to Sawyer in the parking lot and head home with Rowan and Trey.

"I wonder what happened to the people on the stretchers," Rowan says. "Do you think they were murdered?"

Trey frowns. "I don't think paramedics are supposed to move bodies if they're dead. So there must be some hope of them surviving if they're carrying them out to the ambulance." He pauses. "Of course, there could be dead people inside the house."

I look at Tori's description on my phone. "She didn't give us much to go on. I hope she has a chance to text me again soon. 'A house.' That's about all we've got. Hello, this is Chicago, land of many houses."

On Saturday morning I send Tori the longest text known to humankind: *Tori, I think we can help you but we need more information. Can you please answer the questions I asked? Tell us everything you can. Please. The only way to stop the visions from driving you crazy is for you to stop the tragedy from happening. But since you can't, we will do it for you. I'm sure the vision is getting worse every day. Believe me, I understand. I want to help.*

My phone is so silent I think it must be broken. I forward the message to Sawyer just to make sure my phone is actually sending text messages. He replies in a nanosecond: *Good job.*

The hours crawl by as we go out as a family to look at some houses for rent. By midafternoon my parents think they've found the one they want. Even though the rent is a little higher than they'd planned, it's really close to our pile of ashes, and I guess they find that comforting. They go back and forth in quiet voices about the rent being seventy dollars a month higher than they had budgeted based on the insurance money, and after ten minutes of that I want to butt in and tell them I'll give them the stupid seventy bucks a month . . . except I forgot I no longer have a job.

But then, in a flash of brilliance, I remember the envelope Mr. Polselli gave me yesterday. When we get back to Aunt Mary's I race to the living room, pull it from my backpack, and present it to my dad. "This is from the teachers at school," I say.

With a puzzled look on his face, he opens the envelope and pulls out a wad of twenties. He counts the money—all eight hundred dollars of it.

"Holy moly," I say. I feel so weird about it. Teachers

don't have a lot of extra cash. I bet most of them sacrificed something pretty important in order to chip in, like, I don't know, bifocals or cat food or whatever teachers buy.

"That's incredibly generous," Mom says. Her eyes are shining.

And my dad grips the cash like somebody just threw him a lifeline.

Sixteen

On Saturday night Sawyer comes over, and Dad still doesn't yell at him, not even when I say we're going out for a while. Together. Alone.

"Definite progress," Sawyer says later in the car. "Is he just distracted, or do you think he's actually starting to like me?"

I grin. "I wouldn't go that far. I think it's a combination of having too many other things to worry about plus realizing the inevitable—that I'm going to see you whether or not he approves. I think he's given up. At least for now. And as long as I behave."

Sawyer gives me a sidelong glance and slides his hand on my thigh. "Oh?"

And just like that, my whole body tingles. It's been a

while since Sawyer and I have had some time alone. I try to swallow the instant desire in my throat but it rushes up again. "I guess what he doesn't know won't hurt him."

I lean toward Sawyer and watch him driving, the outline of his profile lit up by streetlights. I resist the urge to trace my finger down his sexy chin, run my hand through his thick, dark hair.

He turns to look at me. His lips part when he sees my face, and I hear him take in a short breath. "Jesus, Jules," he says, and his grip on my thigh tightens and inches up.

"Pull over," I whisper.

His Adam's apple bobs in response and he peers ahead, looking for a place to stop. He pulls into the parking lot of a closed factory and parks in the shadows of the building.

I unlatch my seat belt and climb over the gearshift to straddle Sawyer's lap as he adjusts the driver's seat as far back as he can. And then I'm touching his face, nipping his lip with my teeth, drawing the tip of my tongue across his. His seat belt unlatches and I slide it out from between our pressed bodies, between our hot lips, and fling it aside, barely flinching as the buckle hits the window.

Sawyer kisses me hard, and when I move my lips to his neck he moans and reaches up under my shirt, his cool hands on my bare sides, and I can't think, I can only breathe and taste his skin and fumble with the buttons on his shirt with fingers that are shaking. Finally I rest my face against his hot bare chest and imagine us naked together. For the first time, it doesn't seem too weird. A thrill rushes through me from my thighs to my throat. I guide his hand up my side and press it against my bra, and through the fabric his thumb stumbles over my nipple. I suck in a breath.

"Oh, God," he says, and his body convulses under me. I bury my face in his neck and kiss him, run my tongue along his collarbone and my fingers up and down his sides under his shirt. He adjusts again and I grip the waist of his jeans and kiss him full on the mouth as he pushes against me, breathing hard. His hands pull me toward him and he searches with blind fingers for the clasp of my bra.

"It's two hooks in the back," I whisper, my lips against his ear. I don't even know what I'm saying, only that I want him to succeed, I want him to touch me. He finds the clasp and wrestles with it until I help him, and then his hands are cupping my breasts and his hips are grinding, pushing up against me, and I feel mostly euphoric and a little scared as something deep inside me builds.

I rake in a breath and move my jeans against his, like I'm controlled by some other force of nature, and then Sawyer's breath turns ragged and he wraps his arms around me and holds me to him, thrusting his hips and gripping mine, and I find his rhythm and try to match it, feeling weird about it but also wondering if this is a little bit like what it would be like if there weren't any clothes between us. But I don't want to stop and analyze that now.

Waves of lust rush through me and I want to be closer to him, touching him, my body becoming one with his body. I open a few buttons of my shirt, as much as I feel comfortable with, and press my chest against his, roll my hips with him, and I feel so beautiful and free. His breathing grows deeper, heavier, and it's thrilling and scary all at the same time to watch him react to me in this way.

But then he buries his face in my shirt and gasps, "Oh. Oh, shit. Oh, shit. Oh, SHIT." And then his torso jerks and shudders and his gasp turns into a low moan. "Oooh. Faaahck."

I don't know for sure what's happening at first, but even though I'm not an anatomy expert, I think I have an idea. I ease back against the steering wheel and peer at him. "Are you okay?"

His eyes are closed and there's a pained look on his face. "Shit," he groans, and lets his head fall back against the seat. He brings his hand up to cover his eyes, takes a deep breath, and lets it out. "God, Jules. I'm so sorry. I didn't even know that could . . . you know, happen, without actually, you know. Touching it."

I bite my lip, not sure what to do now. Sawyer shifts and gingerly slides his hand into his jeans. He cringes. "Well, that's awkward," he mutters. I ease off his lap and back into my seat, twist my jeans back into place, turn aside, and hook my bra. My lips tingle. I button up my shirt. And I'm not exactly the Sahara Desert in my pants either.

I'm not sure how I'm supposed to feel about what just happened. Flattered? Disgusted? I definitely don't feel disgusted. I feel . . . smarter. Like I'm beginning to figure things out. Applying book knowledge to real life, like Mr. Polselli says, except, ew, let's not think about him right now. But I like knowing what happens. I like knowing how things work. Cause and effect. That's probably weird, isn't it? But I feel like if I understand what's going on with this whole sex thing, I can figure out how much of it I want to take part in, and I can plan better.

I glance at Sawyer to see if he's done doing whatever needed to be done. He's buttoning up his shirt. And then, from his still reclined position, he lolls his head sideways and gives me a sheepish grin. "That was not in the plan," he says. "I'm sorry." He raises his seat back to an upright position. "So, um, basically," he says, like he needs to explain, "I don't know if you are aware of this, but being within, like, fifty feet of you makes me want to have sex with you pretty much all the time. I think that's normal. And I guess even just the hotness and nearness of you combined with the amount of, um, friction and stimulation that occurred," he continues in a scientific voice, his face flushing, "through no fewer than two hearty layers of denim protection, well . . . I guess that was enough to just wake everybody up down there and have 'em throw a party."

I laugh. "No need for sorry." I kind of want to ask him how it felt, but I'm too self-conscious.

He sits up and reaches out to smooth my hair. His fingers linger on my jawbone, and he says, "I love you, Jules, and not just because you make my thing happy. I love you because you make *me* happy."

I grin.

He goes on. "I don't want to push you into having sex, and I don't want to push myself into it either. And I don't want to do it until we are both ready for that, and I don't know when that is, but I'm pretty sure it's not today. So I hope you can forgive me for letting things get a little out of hand."

He chuckles at his pun, and then grows serious again. "I mean it about the love thing, Jules. And I know it's true, because every time I think about you getting hurt trying to stop one of these visions . . ." He drops his gaze. "Well, I can't stand it. I can't lose you. I can't."

My eyes well up. And the thing that is so big inside my chest spreads through my body. I have never felt like this before. I lean over and kiss him softly, gently, on the lips.

And then I smile and sit up and pat him on the chest. "Dude," I say, "I just have to tell you that you buttoned your shirt wrong."

Which, in JuleSawyer language, means "I love you, too. Maybe even forever."

Seventeen

When Sawyer drops me off, I go inside and find Rowan sitting at the table playing Clue Junior with the three younger cousins. She gives me the stink-eye. I wipe my chapped lips with the back of my hand to hide my grin and hope I don't look like I've just been tumbling around a steamed-up vehicle with my bra undone for the past forty-five minutes.

"Where's Trey?" I ask.

"On a date." Rowan clips the words.

"Oh, cool. What about Mom and Dad?" I ask.

Rowan replies through clenched teeth, "On a date."

I laugh.

"I'm serious," Rowan says. "It's like Trey inspired them. After you left, Mom said they haven't been on a date in twenty years, and she made Dad go. Then Aunt Mary decided she and Uncle Vito haven't had a date in eighteen years, so they left too." She smiles evilly at the kids. "Nick was supposed to babysit."

"Where'd Nick go?"

Rowan glares, one eyebrow arched. "On. A. Date."

"Oh my." I snort.

"Yeah." She looks at her cards and writes something down. "So why are you home so early?"

"Um . . ." I try to think of something other than *Sawyer spooged his pants so we called it a night.* "I don't know. Probably because I could feel your agony."

Rowan laughs.

The cousins look at me like I'm a jerk. "She's not in agony," the oldest of the three announces. "She's having fun, aren't you, Ro?"

"Pssh. Yeah, of course. Tons. Gosh, Jules."

"Sorry." I retreat to the living room, stare at my phone, where I have no messages from Tori, and pick up one of the library books and try to read it. I have a little trouble concentrating on the story, though, since I keep thinking about Sawyer and getting this goofy smile on my face. I'm kind of pathetic right now. Even the cousins' yelling doesn't bother me.

A half hour later Rowan makes everybody go to bed. She comes into the living room and sits on the piano bench next to my chair. And she's all business. "Any word from Tori?"

"No." *In fact, I kind of forgot all about her for a while.*

"You should call her."

"But her mom might see it's me."

"Call the room phone. I'll call, in case her mom answers. She doesn't know my voice."

I tilt my head. "Well, that's a brilliant idea."

"See?" she says, stretching into a yawn. "This is why you need me."

"Isn't it too late to call?"

"It's, like, nine fifteen on a Saturday night. Don't be ridiculous."

"But she's not exactly able to be out having fun."

"Stop stalling."

"Fine." I look up the number for the hospital and give Tori's room number to Rowan.

She calls, and after a listening for a second, punches in the room number. She looks at me. "Ringing," she whispers. Then her eyes light up. "Hi there, Tori?" She waits. "Oh, sorry. Is Tori able to come to the phone? This is her friend Rowan from UC." Rowan pauses, then gives me a thumbs-up. She lowers her voice. "Hi, Tori, this is Jules's sister. We know you can't talk because of your mom. Maybe now would be a good time to smile or laugh like I said something funny."

Rowan pauses. "Yes, your head hurts because of the visions and we can help you stop them if you just tell us what's happening. Is there a good time for me to come by to see you when your mom isn't there?"

Rowan listens for a minute. Her face grows puzzled. "Oh. I see. Maybe you could e-mail—what's that?" Rowan frowns. "You're welcome. Wait. Hello?" She looks at me. "She said she had to go and hung up."

"Nice going, Demarco."

"Shut it," Rowan warns. She hops off the piano bench and lies down on the living room floor, splaying her limbs in all directions. "She must really be under some kind of freaky surveillance over there."

"I told you. Her mom is really protective. She rarely leaves."

"Clearly."

I don't know what else to do but wait. All I know is that some people in a house in Chicago—presumably—are going to be hurting pretty soon.

When Trey and Ben walk in, Rowan and I look at Ben. And then we both look at each other. And I turn back to Ben and say, "Help me, Obi-Wan Galang. You're my only hope."

Eighteen

Trey, Ben, Rowan, and I decide to brainstorm before the parentals begin to trickle in, but we can't come up with anything that we haven't already thought of. We determine that Ben could go visit Tori, but they still wouldn't be able to talk about anything.

"What if I bring her a notebook and hide questions in the middle of it?" Ben suggests.

"Her mom will see her answering," Trey says. He slips his hand into Ben's. "Nice idea, though." Ben smiles at Trey, and all around the world millions of puppies are caught being almost as adorable as them.

I flop back in my chair. "I think all we can do is wait. The more things we try, the bigger risk there is that Mrs. Hayes will confiscate Tori's phone. We just need to chill.

I feel like I need medication to get through this. Or some comic relief."

Ben picks up one of the cousins' picture books and starts reading to us. I forgot how hilarious some picture books are. The laughter takes the pressure off the Tori situation, and by the time Uncle Vito walks in, yelling, "Hey, it's the Filipino!" we're already in various fits of giggles over this book about a bear who wants his hat back.

Ben leaves around midnight—I sneak a peek of him and Trey kissing in the driveway—and our parents stay out even later. Trey has stars in his eyes, and finally, when Rowan can't take all the blooming love any longer, she wakes up her long-distance boyfriend, Charlie, who lives in Manhattan, and Face Times with him. He's funny when he's sleepy. Or maybe everything is funny tonight so that it doesn't have to be tragic.

I drift off eventually, my bones aching from sleeping on this hard living room floor for almost a week, and when I wake up, it's still dark, and my phone is vibrating with a text message.

2 bodies outside w/ambulance, 2 inside dead, no blood, no house number, Loomis St. OMG my head! Visions everywhere I look, sirens wailing, won't stop. Can you help me?

I look at the time. Six fifteen in the morning. And I remember when I was in the hospital after the meatball truck crash. Right around 6:00 a.m.—that's when they come to poke you and hand out meds and check your temperature. Maybe Mrs. Hayes sleeps through it. I text back quickly, trying to be really encouraging: *Great info! This helps a lot! Are there any clues about what day this happens? And what time—sunny, cloudy? Look hard. I know it sucks. You're doing great! What else is nearby? What's the house made of? Color/style? 1 story or 2?*

And then I wait. Again.

I manage to get a couple more hours of sleep, waking up only when I hear Mom and Dad leave for mass. Trey is up too, eating cereal. I show him the text, and he gets on his phone immediately, looking up Loomis Street.

"Did she say North or South Loomis?"

"She just said Loomis. I'll ask her to look again."

Trey scrolls down his screen, again and again. "It's a really long street."

I lean over to see. Trey zooms in and scrolls. "Lots of houses. Like, miles of them. See if she can narrow down what side of the street it's on. And we really need a house number or at least a cross street."

I doubt I can get any of that info out of her. "I'll ask," I say. I start a new text with these additional questions and send it. "She said she sees visions everywhere she looks. That's not a good sign."

"Is that because we haven't figured things out?"

"Well, Loomis is a big clue. If the vision is still constant and not letting up, I think that means . . . it's imminent."

"Crap," Trey mutters. "That's what I thought."

We look at each other, both thinking the same thing. *We're not going to make it.*

Nineteen

Tori doesn't respond, and she doesn't respond, and she doesn't respond. On Sunday afternoon Sawyer, Rowan, Trey, Ben, and I pile into Sawyer's car and we find Loomis Street. We drive up it slowly. There are nice sections of Loomis Street and not so nice sections. I take notes on the kinds of houses on the street in hopes that Tori will give me a clue, and I text her again. *Big or small? Nice or run-down? Brick or siding?* Anything. ANYTHING.

If we only knew how the people died, we might be able to go door-to-door . . . or something. Send out a flyer warning of a homicidal maniac on the loose or whatever. But there's nothing more to work with.

By Tuesday we're all really on edge.

By Wednesday we're freaking out.

On Thursday we break down and send Ben to visit her, just to make sure Tori didn't die or something. We sit around our spot at the library and wait for Ben to call. When he finally does, Trey runs outside so they can talk, and we all follow.

Trey puts Ben on speakerphone.

"Okay," Trey says. "We're all here and you're on speaker."

"Hey, everybody," Ben says. His voice has lost the funny/sarcastic edge for the moment, which does not reassure me in any way. "I went to the hospital and tried to see Tori. The nurse stopped me at the door and said I should wait, that Tori wasn't feeling well today but maybe I could go in after her meds kicked in. So I waited. After about an hour, I figured everybody had forgotten about me in the waiting room, so I snuck back down the hallway and tried to peek in the window to her room but the shade was drawn. Still, I could hear something in there. So I was really quiet and I opened the door a crack, and all I could hear was Tori moaning over and over, 'Make it stop! Make it stop!' and her mother on the phone yelling at somebody, telling them to come immediately or she'd sue for malpractice."

There's a pause while we let the words sink in. Finally Trey says, "Holy shit."

"Yeah," says Ben.

"What happened? Did you get caught?" Rowan asks.

"No. I closed the door and slipped away. I didn't want them to see me in case you guys need me to do something else."

I catch Trey's eye and grin despite the situation. Ben is definitely a keeper.

"Okay," I say, realizing everybody's looking to me to call the next play. "Great job, Ben. Seriously. We couldn't do this without you. Thank you. I guess . . . I guess we just wait. I don't know what else to do. We have no date or time, no exact location, not even a reasonable vicinity." A sense of doom descends over me, and unexpected emotion clogs my throat. "So, I don't know." My voice squeaks at the end, and Sawyer and Rowan both put their arms around me. "I guess I failed on this one."

"Stop it," Trey says, and his eyes flash. "You didn't fail. The victim failed you. It's not your fault. We are not God." He pauses. "Or dog."

I half smile through watery eyes and nod. But I can't help it. I still feel like a failure.

The next morning, as I'm drying my hair, Sawyer texts me. *I'm outside the front door. Can you come out?*

I set down the hair dryer with a clatter, slip past Rowan, and run down the hallway and through the dining room and kitchen and breezeway, and fling open the door. I go outside in my bare feet to Sawyer.

Sawyer, with the thick hair and green eyes and ropy lashes.

Sawyer, the boy I love.

Sawyer, who is holding a newspaper.

He looks at me, solemn, wordless. And he points.

I don't want to look. But I do it anyway.

On the local news page, one headline reads: TWO DEAD, TWO CRITICAL FROM CARBON MONOXIDE POISONING NEAR ADA PARK.

I look at him. My lip starts trembling. "Are you sure it's the right house?"

He nods. And then he reads for me, "'Emergency response teams were called to a home on South Loomis Street late last night after a Boston man's repeated, unsuccessful attempts to reach his sister and brother-in-law and their elderly parents. The older couple were pronounced dead at the scene, and the younger man and woman remain in critical condition. It is unknown . . .'" Sawyer trails off. He lets his arms drop heavily and looks at me.

". . . if they'll survive," I say softly, finishing the report. I sink to the step and bury my face in my hands. Sawyer sits next to me and wraps his arms around me. But I cannot be consoled.

Twenty

By the time I look up, Sawyer has magically summoned Rowan and Trey, and they're staring at the news like they can't believe it. And then they say it. "I can't believe it." And I almost want to shake them, because I told them this would happen. They know this. But they don't understand the coarse reality of the visions like I do. Like Sawyer does.

I collect my racing thoughts and stand up. "I need to get ready." Without another word, I march inside and finish my hair, feeling numb. Those people could've been fine. That man in a distant city, so concerned about his sister, his parents, that he called 911. That man who has to bury not only both parents at once, but also grieve for his sister and brother-in-law, who could die any minute.

That man could've been fine too, going about his business, but not now.

All this because Tori wouldn't tell me the information I needed. And I realize that if I'd only known the cause of death, we could have gone door-to-fucking-door up and down Loomis Street with a carbon monoxide detector a *week* ago, and saved their lives.

"It would have been so *easy!*" I yell at myself in the mirror, and I slam down the brush and take off down the hallway, shoving past Nick and Rowan on my way to grab my backpack, and then I go outside, where Sawyer still remains like I knew he would, waiting for me. I climb into his car and we go to school like good little students, and all day my fury grows. And grows. Kind of like the fire that burned down my family's life. And I'm not sure if I can contain it.

After school I don't even have to say it—it's like Sawyer can read my mind.

"You want to visit Tori?" he asks.

"Yes, please."

And without trying to stop me or suggest I wait a day until my anger dies down, he drives me to the UC hospital. And I am so furious I can't wait for the elevator, so I take the stairs two at a time, and Sawyer follows. We go down the hallway to Tori's room, and for a split second I worry that maybe she's not there. Maybe she's been discharged, and I won't get to yell at her after all.

But my split second of worry is for nothing, because when I get to her room and open the door, there she is, sitting up, talking to her mother. Looking beautiful. I want to kill her.

They look up at me when I come in, and I almost falter, but I can feel Sawyer right behind me, and I know I have to do this. For me. For that poor man and his family. Then I almost falter again when I realize I forgot to bring the newspaper in, but Sawyer slaps it into my hand just before I make an ass of myself, and I walk over to Tori with it and shove it in her face. "Does this look familiar?" I ask, pointing to the photo of the house with the ambulance outside. I shake the paper a little to get her to look at it instead of me.

Mrs. Hayes gets to her feet and starts pointing at me, protesting my presence, but then she catches the look on Tori's face and stops. She goes to look at the article too.

As I watch the look of horror grow in Tori's eyes, I start to shake. "You did this," I say in a low voice. I look at Mrs. Hayes. "It's your fault they died."

They are stunned. "Is that the house you . . . you saw?" Mrs. Hayes asks Tori.

She nods. She won't look at me.

Mrs. Hayes will, though. "The vision is gone," she says. "It's over."

I want to punch her in the face. "That's because *this*

happened! There's no saving anybody now. They're dead! You both had the power to help stop this, but you didn't help. You didn't believe me. You wouldn't let Tori talk to me." I stop to breathe, to try to keep my voice low so no one comes in.

"I couldn't see my phone screen anymore to read your texts or respond," Tori says, distressed. "Plus, I was so sick from the constant movement. But now it's gone. No more vision." It's like she doesn't grasp what happened.

"Tori," I say. "Listen to me. If Sawyer had done what you did—if he hadn't believed me, or had refused to do anything about what he was seeing, *like you did with your vision*, you would be dead. You. Would be dead. And ten others in that music room *would also be dead*. You are alive because Sawyer acted on his vision. These people are dead because you wouldn't act on yours." I slap the newspaper. "Do you get it now? Do you?"

Sawyer puts his hand on my shoulder and I stop talking. Tori weeps into her hand, teardrops falling between her fingers onto the newspaper.

Mrs. Hayes at least has the dignity not to kick me out. But I don't need any encouragement to leave. I've had enough. And I think I said enough. Probably just a little too much.

On the way home my anger begins to subside. But

there's still something that infuriates me. Something I can't let go of.

"Her vision," I say after a while, "it just went away. Just like it did for us after we risked our lives. Only she didn't have to risk anything except motion sickness and her mom being mad at her."

Sawyer nods. He's worn a thoughtful expression since we left the hospital. "I noticed that. I'm not sure what I think about it either. Like, I should feel relieved, but really I'm kind of pissed off about it." He drums the steering wheel with his thumb. "It sure might have been easier to just ride it out and pretend like people weren't dying. If we'd only known . . ."

I look at him. "It wouldn't have been easier for me."

The corner of his mouth twitches and his eyes don't leave the road. He reaches over and takes my hand.

Twenty-One

I don't want to go to my aunt Mary's. I don't want to talk to anyone. I feel bad that I'm ignoring Trey and Rowan when I know they're probably reeling from all of this too, but I can't help it—I need an escape right now. It's like everything's closing in on me and I can't breathe. Sawyer takes me to his cousin Kate's apartment. She's not home.

It's a cute little place near the community college where she goes to school. Two tiny bedrooms and an even tinier bathroom. But a big kitchen. Isn't that how every home should be?

"Sit," Sawyer says with an Italian accent, sounding eerily like his grandfather Fortuno, magistrate of the evil Angotti empire. "I cook for you."

I grin for the first time in days, sit down on the sofa, and relax, reading Kate's fashion magazines while Sawyer bangs around in the kitchen. I text my mom so she knows where I am. And it occurs to me just how much more freedom I've had since the restaurant burned down. Not only because I don't have to report for my job but also because my parents have had too much stuff on their minds to keep up their reign of terror over us. Our whole family has been forced to adapt, and that part, at least, has been in my favor.

I look up and watch Sawyer cook, and I think how wonderful it is that we have this thing in common. How we learned to feed people from our parents, and they learned from their parents and grandparents, and so on down the line. Sawyer hasn't spoken about his parents since he moved out. I guess I've been hogging all the attention these days.

"Have you seen your parents lately?" I ask.

"I stopped in to see my mom the other day. She's fine."

"That's good. I bet she was glad to see you."

"Yeah." He doesn't elaborate, and I don't press him on it. I can tell he doesn't want to talk about them.

"So," Sawyer says after a while, "do you think your father still has visions? Or do you think he had one and it stopped after its tragedy happened, like Tori's did?"

I've been thinking about that. "I guess I don't know. I

mean, I believe he's had one for sure, obviously. But . . . I don't know." I frown, puzzled. Something doesn't add up.

"Maybe it's not a repeating vision that's been driving his depression all this time," Sawyer says lightly, pulling toasted raviolis from the broiler and plating them with a small bowl of marinara and freshly grated cheese—from here it looks and smells like Pecorino Romano, but I'm not sure. "Maybe it's the guilt of not having saved people."

I think about that. And I don't know. I might never know.

But I do know that I'm hungry and this bad boy in the kitchen can cook.

When Sawyer drives me home, I invite him to come inside. And he does. He offers a nervous hello when I officially introduce him to Aunt Mary and Uncle Vito, but they greet him with warmth. When my mom comes up to him, he plants a kiss on her cheek, which makes her smile, and my dad doesn't yell or kick him out. He just leaves. Probably heading to the ash heap to find some more treasures. I still think that's progress. The Sawyer part, not the treasures part.

Once Sawyer and I migrate to the living room with Trey and Rowan, I ask them, feeling a little ashamed, "You guys doing okay? I'm really sorry I blasted out of here."

"It's just weird," Rowan says. "I feel so bad."

Trey nods. "It sucks. It's like we had this power to do something good, and we didn't use it."

"Not *didn't*," Sawyer says. "*Couldn't*. We did our best. We did everything we could think of to stop it. But we can't force some stranger to give us what we need."

"And now it's over," I say softly. I still can't believe it. "I mean, I think so. There's nobody for Tori to pass the vision curse to."

"Tori told us the vision is completely gone," Sawyer explains, and he fills in the others on our visit.

And it's a boring Friday night for the first time in forever. None of us are working. There's no vision to ponder. Ben shows up after a while and we all hang out in Aunt Mary's living room, even the cousins, and we play this game called Apples to Apples, and after months of stress, it's like I'm finally starting to decompress. It's over.

It's really over.

When my dad comes home around nine, he doesn't have pocketfuls of scavenged burned junk. He has ice chests and ice and bags of groceries. We stop our game and look up as he stands in the kitchen, arms laden.

"Two things," he says in his old familiar, booming voice, and it shocks me to hear it again after so long. "First, our new landlord just called and said we don't have to wait until the fifteenth—the house is ready and we can move in on Sunday."

We try not to cheer too loudly because we don't want to seem ungrateful, but we are all ecstatic over this news.

"And second," Dad continues, holding up a bag of groceries, "Paula and I are taking Demarco's Food Truck out tomorrow. And next week, and the next, and every day until we open the doors of our new, improved restaurant!"

The household breaks into applause, and I cheer too, at first, until the doubt creeps in and all I can do is clasp my hands together and stare at my dad's flushed cheeks and triumphant smile, and wait for the cracks to come back and ruin it all.

Twenty-Two

Mom and Dad start preparing the sauce on Aunt Mary's stove for tomorrow's big day in the meatball truck. We go back to our game, eventually forfeiting so the little kids win, because Aunt Mary says they have to go to bed as soon as the game is over, and we just want to get rid of them because we're selfish teenagers like that.

Nick sticks around and hangs out with us because all his friends are working tonight. He doesn't say much. We don't really have anything in common, even though he's between Trey and me in age and we played together a lot when we were little. We haven't been close since I started elementary school, even when he spent an occasional day working for the restaurant.

So things are somewhat quiet, and we can't talk about

what happened with the vision even if we want to. And strangely, I don't want to. I snuggle into Sawyer and he drapes his arm over my shoulders, and it feels wonderful to be safe and stress free for once.

I think about the man who has to bury his parents. I look up at Sawyer and murmur, "Should we go to the funeral?" And I love that he immediately knows what I'm talking about.

"We can do that. I'll try to find out when it is."

I nod. He smiles.

When I get a text message, I look at my phone. "It's from Tori," I say. I open it and read: *I'm so sorry.*

That's all there is.

I raise an eyebrow and mutter, "Jules is not impressed." I shove the phone back into my pocket.

"What was that?" Sawyer says near my ear.

"Tori says she's sorry."

"Good. Maybe she understands it now. What did you say back?"

I grunt.

Sawyer shifts so he can look at my face. "Jules," he says, "I know how you feel, but there are a few factors here that you're not really considering. One, she couldn't see the phone screen because of the vision playing out on it. Two, her mother dictates absolutely everything."

"Her mother ought to be the one saying sorry," I mutter.

"And three," Sawyer continues in a louder voice, pretending he didn't hear me, "Tori has been heavily medicated this entire time. Do you even remember when you were on your pain medication in the hospital? Do you happen to recall Trey on pain meds?"

"I do," Ben offers from across the room. "He was . . . *emboldened*."

"Whoa," Trey says. "We agreed not to talk about that."

I glance at Nick, who is playing some game on his phone and ignoring us.

"Anyway," Sawyer says, "you can't judge her equally with someone who can actually stay awake for a four-hour stretch and doesn't appear to be stoned all hours of the day and night."

I sigh. "You're right, I know. I just don't want to forgive her."

"That's up to you, I guess," Sawyer says.

"Yes, it is," I say. But I know Sawyer is the one being reasonable here. "I'm sorry," I say. "I'll think about it."

Dad and Mom say they can't afford to hire us to help them quite yet. We say we'll work for free, but it's like they're having some sort of weird bonding time or something and they don't want us along. So while they head off to the public market Saturday morning, Trey bolts for the shower, and Rowan and I are supposed to pack.

"Pack what?" Rowan asks from the middle of the living room floor, where she's sitting like a pretzel with her hair all messed up from sleep. She's cranky. "We don't own anything."

I look around the living room, realizing we've managed to collect a good deal of stuff since the fire. "I don't know. All this stuff, I guess."

"What are we supposed to put it in?" she whines.

I glare at her. "How about we shove it in your face hole?"

"How about we cram it up your butt . . . nose."

We stare each other down. Finally I concede. "Buttnose is funny."

"Thank you. It was an accident."

"Oh, really?"

"You can cut the sarcasm." She gets up and kicks me in the shin with her bare foot.

I snort my mockery in her direction.

She kicks me again and I grab her by the back of the neck and shove her to the couch and sit on her.

She pokes her fingers at me, trying to find a sensitive spot, so I'm forced to bounce up and down on her while giving her a noogie. Then she hits her mark. "Whoa!" I yell, and jump off of her. "Out of bounds, loser. That was totally my buttnose."

She sits up and smooths her hair, trying not to laugh.

I back my way toward the kitchen in case she plans to try something else, and scrounge around for some shopping bags to pack our junk in.

Somewhere during the scuffle I got another text from Tori. I glance at it: *I really am sorry and I need to talk to you.*

I groan and shove the phone back into my pocket. "Great. Tori's feeling guilty now," I call out to Rowan. I skirt a small cousin in the dining room and head back to the living room with the bags. I throw a few at Rowan's head.

"How can you tell?" she asks.

"She just sent me another text. Says she really is sorry and that she wants to talk."

Rowan puts her clothes into a bag. "What did you tell her?"

"I haven't responded."

She shrugs. "She's probably trying to deal with the shock of it."

I feel a twinge in my gut, but I'm not giving in. "She could have prevented all of this."

"Yeah, I think she probably knows that now," Rowan says with a smirk.

"How would you know? You don't even know her."

"It's a logical guess. Besides, you two aren't exactly BFFs either."

"Yeah we are. We're BFFs. I know everything she's thinking and you know nothing."

Rowan rolls her eyes. "I'm just saying you're not being very gracious. She practically died. This is a lot to take on from a hospital bed."

I put my index finger in the air. "But! She didn't die. Because Sawyer and I risked our lives for her. And she did not do the same for her fellow humans of Chicago."

Rowan sighs and gives up. And for some reason I don't feel very triumphant about my win.

Twenty-Three

Sunday is a day of joy. We have a new place. Not just an apartment—a whole little house in a neighborhood across from my old elementary school. And there's no restaurant attached. It'll be months at least before I have to go to school smelling like pizza. Mean people will cease to recognize me. I may survive high school after all.

Ben and Sawyer show up at the new place, surprising us with a pickup truck full of used furniture. My dad stares from the garage (yes, we have a little garage!) as they start unloading it onto the driveway (because yes, we have a driveway, too!), and walks over to them.

"What's all this?" Dad says.

"We brought you some furniture," Ben says. "Thought you could use it. Is it okay if we show you what's here?"

Dad's stern gaze sweeps over the scene.

"You don't have to keep any of it," Sawyer replies. He stops unloading, looking uncertain. "We just thought . . ." He wipes a bead of sweat from his temple and stops talking, likely scared to death.

My dad shakes the hard look off his face and clears his throat. "We can use it. At least for a little while until our new stuff comes." He lifts his chin slightly. "Thank you." But we all know our "new stuff" hasn't even been decided on, much less ordered. We're being extra cautious with the insurance money since we don't know how long it'll take to get the new restaurant running.

I leave Sawyer outside to bond with Dad (har har) and follow Rowan into our new bedroom, where we each currently have two bags of clothes and toiletries and basically nothing else. We will have new beds to assemble later today, and I'm hoping there's a dresser on that pickup truck.

"Where'd they get all that stuff?" Rowan asks.

"No idea," I say. I'm not sure I want to know.

By evening, the house is starting to feel like a home, and the best part is that there are no little cousins running around. It's a little bit bigger than our old apartment above the restaurant. Or at least, it feels that way without all the piles of junk. I worry that this place will fill up too. And I don't know how to prevent that from happening, but I'm sure as hell going to try.

Sawyer returns later in his car, having taken the truck away, to see if we want him to pick up some burgers, and then he's gone again with our orders. When he returns with the food, I watch him as he ever so slowly works his way into the good graces of my dad. And I think that makes Sawyer a good, quality guy. I will just have to keep him.

Before Sawyer heads home for the night, he and I sit together in the dark on the front step of my new house, and he tells me that he found an updated article about the carbon monoxide poisoning. He says the old couple who died were both receiving hospice care, which means that they were already dying. And that the man's sister is fine now, and her husband is improving and should be okay.

I'm quiet for a moment. And then I say reluctantly, "It doesn't excuse what Tori did, but I guess that's a pretty good outcome under the circumstances."

"You know, there's a chance that this even spared the old people from a pretty miserable ending to their lives," Sawyer says. "I mean, I don't know that for sure. But it's possible. And maybe it's okay to think of it that way."

"Maybe," I say. "Is there a funeral planned?"

"Just a private memorial service for the family."

"Well. I guess that's that." I draw in a deep breath of

the fresh spring nighttime air in my new yard (because I have a yard!) and I blow it out, trying to get rid of all the anger that was stored up inside me. I imagine it escaping my lungs and leaving my fingertips. And it feels like all the negative crap is finally beginning to clear out.

"It's like a fresh start," I say, more to myself than to Sawyer. "We have a nice new home. My dad is getting out of bed every day. The parentals are back to work with the meatball truck. I no longer smell like pizza. We experimented with sexy time."

Sawyer laughs. "Is that what we're calling it?"

"Yeah."

"And let's not forget that there are no more visions to deal with."

I smile in the darkness. "Right on," I say. I squeeze his hand and he squeezes back. And for the briefest of moments, I feel like all is well in the world.

When my phone vibrates, I am reluctant to pull it out of my pocket for fear of disturbing this new perfect universe. And when I see who's calling, I'm tempted to ignore her. But I don't. Maybe it's because the old people were already dying, and maybe it's because I'm feeling fresh and full of love, and maybe it's because I know deep down I've been too hard on her, but this time I decide to answer.

"Hi, Tori," I say.

"I'm so sorry," she says. She's crying.

"I know. I get it. It's in the past."

"No," she says. "Let me explain—"

I sigh. She needs to say things. She needs to help herself heal. I can handle that. "Go ahead."

And for the second time in a month, three little words change everything. "Jules," she says, her voice faltering, "it's happening again."

Twenty-Four

My mind doesn't compute what Tori is saying.

"Hold on," I say. "I'm putting you on speaker so Sawyer can listen too, okay?"

"Okay."

Sawyer's face is a question. I press the button. "Go ahead. Start from where you said 'It's happening again.'"

"Well, it is. And I'm so sorry—"

"I know you're sorry," I say impatiently. "What do you mean—are you seeing the vision again? How is that possible?"

"It's not the same one," she says. "It's a new one now. Totally different."

"What?" Sawyer covers his face with his hands and shakes his head slowly, swearing under his breath.

"Wait. How are you suddenly allowed to talk to me

now?" I demand. "What about your mother?"

"She's right here—she's the one who made me call you. I knew you'd be mad, but—and she's sorry too. She wants me to tell you that."

I roll my eyes to Jesus in the sky. "Sure. Of course. You're both sorry now. Little late for that."

"I *know*," she says. "Just please, you have to help us. I promise we'll do everything right this time. I mean it! My mom says she won't interfere."

I stand up and start pacing along the sidewalk. What am I supposed to do here? Say no? I can't. I'm ethically bound. Personally responsible.

I close my eyes and rub my left temple, where a sudden headache has sprung up.

"Jules?"

"I'm still here," I say. "I'm just processing."

"Sorry."

She needs to stop saying *that* now too. I take a breath and blow it out, and then sink back to my spot on the step. "Okay. When did this start?"

"Saturday, I guess."

"Is that why you sent me the apology text message?" My blood starts to boil.

"No, I sent that text on Friday night. I swear. I feel terrible about the people dying. I wish I could go back in time and fix it. I mean it."

Sawyer pats my knee. "Let it go, Demarco," he whispers.

I shoot him a look, but I know he's right.

With a whoosh of air from my lungs, I let it go. "All right. Tell me what's happening. Sawyer's going to take notes on his phone, so please try to be very specific about everything." I glance at Sawyer, who quickly gets his phone out. "Let's hear it."

"Okay," she says, and I hear her mom saying something encouraging in the background. "There's a ship."

"A ship?" both Sawyer and I exclaim. We look at each other in alarm. "Wait. Where? In Chicago?"

"I—I don't know. It's in the water. It looks like the ocean."

"The ocean?" Sawyer and I exclaim again. We need to stop doing that.

"I mean, I don't know. There are huge waves and rocks. And the ship is sinking."

This time Sawyer and I are silent. "Are there people on board?" I ask after a pause. *Of course there are, dumb shit.*

"Yes. Lots of people. And they're jumping and sliding and falling off . . ." She chokes on a sob. "Some are hurt. A bunch of them are going to drown."

We are silent.

"The looks on their faces . . . ," Tori says in a near whisper. "The panic and fear . . ."

Sawyer springs to life after the initial shock and starts typing everything into his phone. I wait for him to catch up, and I try to pull my thoughts together.

"How big is the ship?" I ask, my voice more gentle now. I know how horrible it is to see death over and over.

"I don't know. Pretty big. Not like a giant freighter or cruise ship or anything, but yeah. Kind of big."

"What color is it?"

"White. And some blue."

"How many people do you see?"

She's quiet for a long moment, and I think she might be counting. "Twenty or thirty," she says. "It's hard to count them because the scene goes by so fast."

Sawyer mutters an expletive.

"And do they all . . . drown?"

"I—I think so."

"Dear God," I say. I slump against the step and stare blindly at the phone. I can't comprehend. How are we supposed to save that many people? "Hey, Tori?" I say after a minute. "I'm going to have to call you back once I come up with a list of questions for you. Okay?"

"Yeah."

"You okay? I know this is horrible." All my anger toward her and her mother has now evaporated.

"I'm okay," she says. But I hear her crying.

"Tori, if you help us, it's going to be okay. Why are you crying?"

It takes her a minute. And then she says through sobs, "I don't want this to be my fault too."

Twenty-Five

When I hang up, I hear a noise behind me, and for a second I panic. What if my parents heard everything? How would I explain this? But when I turn to look, it's Trey. Rowan's there too, behind him.

"You gave me a heart attack," I say. "How long have you been standing there?"

"I had the bedroom window open and I could hear you guys talking," Rowan says. "So I got Trey and we came out."

"We heard almost the whole thing," Trey says, his voice grim. He glances over his shoulder at the house and says, "Let's take a walk. I'm pulling Ben in on this over the phone if that's okay."

"Yeah, definitely," I say. We head across the street to

the elementary school and walk the sidewalks around the property while Trey updates Ben, and then he keeps him on the line to listen to our conversation.

Sawyer begins by recapping the notes he took. "White-and-blue ship, ocean, high waves, rocks, twenty to thirty people, some injured, in the water, all going to drown." He stumbles and sucks in a breath. "Geez," he mutters, shoving his phone into his pocket.

"You okay?" I ask.

"Yeah. Just . . . just blinded for a minute by the phone's backlight."

I frown, because his breathing is a little too heavy and his hand a little too clammy in mine for that to be the problem. But I push it aside. We need to figure this out.

"Okay," Trey says. "I'm really not excited about this at all. So let's start with this ocean bit. I'm telling you guys right now, we are not going to any freaking ocean. If this thing isn't local, it's out of our hands. That's my decision, and I'm the oldest, and I can, like, vote an' shit, and I'm telling you that this is the way it's going to be." He sounds like he thinks we're going to argue.

"No, you're right," I say. "I'm on board with that." I cringe at the unintended pun. "Anybody want to challenge Trey and his self-appointed authori*tay*? Nobody? Okay." I look at Trey. "Hey, I think you just defined us as being strictly local superheroes."

"There's only so much a superhero with no actual powers can do," Rowan says matter-of-factly.

"And we're a picky, demanding bunch," Sawyer adds, apparently feeling better now. "We put our foot down whenever we decide a tragedy is on the wrong side of the local boundary line."

"*Feet,*" I say. "Our foot? Like we all have one big collective foot?" I shake my head. "I don't think so."

"Thank you, grammar whore," Rowan mutters.

"I also have feet, not foot," Ben contributes through the phone.

Sometimes this is just how we do our best thinking.

We come up with a list of questions and call Tori back. Her phone rings and rings, and finally someone answers—Tori's mother. I get a sick feeling in my stomach, like I'm about to be yelled at, but all she says is that Tori is asleep, and can we maybe text the questions instead?

I agree and she actually thanks me, and we hang up. I start typing.

Five things to ask Tori:

1. Are the rocks in the middle of water or part of a shoreline or what?

2. Do you see any land?

3. Are there any markings on the ship—name, numbers, logos, designs?

4. What's the weather like?

5. Time of day? Sun position?

I look up and show everybody.

"That's enough to start with," Sawyer says. "We don't want to overwhelm her." His uneasy look is back, and I wonder if he's changing his mind about this.

We head back home and stand in the driveway. I make everybody gather around, and I say, "I wish we didn't have to do this, guys. It was so nice there for a couple days, thinking it was all over and we could go on with our lives." I watch Sawyer's face as he stares at the ground. "You can all walk away, you know. This is my deal. And I don't want anybody here who doesn't want to be here. I can't handle that hanging over my head." I look at them. "Think about it and let me know."

"I don't need to think about it," Trey says.

"Me neither," Rowan adds. "I'm in."

"I'll go where Trey goes," Ben says. I forgot he was still on the phone with us.

Sawyer looks up. "We're all in, baby," he says. "Sink or swim." He chuckles uneasily.

Trey groans and pats Sawyer on the back. We say good-bye to Ben and hang up, and make our way to the house. Rowan and I walk together, while Trey and Sawyer fall behind and linger by Sawyer's car. And I hear Trey say, "It'll be okay, bro. We'll get through it together."

I glance at them, puzzled. And I realize Sawyer's not following us to come inside.

"Later, guys," he says. "Night, Jules." He gets into the car, starts it, and pulls out of the driveway. I knit my brows, then lift my hand to wave, and watch him go.

Twenty-Six

In the morning, after the traditional jockeying for the bathroom at 6:00 a.m. (I lose due to phone-checking distraction), I'm relieved to find a lengthy message from Tori:

1. Rocks are in the distance along (I think) the shore.

2. Can't really see much land per se though because of weird angle, spray, and chaos but I think it's there.

3. Ship is mostly white, but blue on bottom. Didn't catch any markings—everything goes so fast.

4. Weather is stormy. I think it's raining but could be spray.

5. Some light low in sky like early midmorning and maybe a glimpse of a far-off building? Could just be a weird shadow. It's just a flicker. Is there a way to stop this crazy thing so I can actually look at it?

I reply: *Great stuff here. Will check in with you soon. We'll teach you how to pause it. Let me know if anything new shows up—it usually does.* As she probably already knows.

There's another text message, from Sawyer this time. *Sorry I left all weird. Wasn't feeling well. Better today. Ready to tackle Tori's vision. See you at school. <3*

I smile. Maybe that's all it was.

At school Sawyer acts completely normal, and I think I must have seen something that wasn't really there regarding his weirdness yesterday. Trey, Sawyer, and I meet up for lunch as usual, and for the first time since the fire, Roxie and BFF Sarah give me a long stare as they walk by our table, and Roxie says something immature about my ugly, hand-me-down fire clothes.

"Ahh," I call after her, "an insult! Finally! Now things are really starting to feel like they're back to normal. I knew I was missing something in my life."

"You're welcome," Roxie says.

Trey and I look at each other. "She was actually funny," he says.

"I was just going to say that," I say. "Jules is impressed!"

"So is Trey," Trey says.

Sawyer looks at us. "Is this the latest Demarco thing to do? I'm just trying to keep up here. I thought we were still doing dot-com jokes."

"Please," I scoff. "Dot-com jokes are so two visions ago. Stay on your toes, Angotti, or you're off the team."

"You can be on my team," Trey tells him with a wink.

Sawyer shakes his head and grins. "Aw, man. I thought Ben would cure you of this desire to force homosexuality on me for your own selfish whims."

"Ben's not here," Trey says. He leans toward Sawyer. "Come on. Kiss kiss. Huh? Yeah?"

Sawyer laughs out loud. "Trey, my friend, if you can keep me from drowning, I'll give you a kiss you'll never forget."

"Aaand, here we go." I fold my arms.

Trey sits back and looks offended. "How dare you, Sawyer. Really. I'd never cheat on Ben."

Sawyer just shakes his head.

I change the subject. "So, what are we going to do about Tori? Should we head over there after school, or what?" I'm personally getting really sick of the drive to UC. The traffic makes me crazy.

Trey and Sawyer sober up and we toss around the options. "There's not a huge hurry, is there? All the visions have had time frames of at least a few weeks, right?" Sawyer asks.

"Yeah. Mine was more like six or seven weeks. Longer than yours," I say.

"And mine was longer than Tori's first one," Sawyer says.

Trey knits his brows. "So it appears that the time from first vision to the day of the tragedy is growing progressively shorter. I wonder if that's something to note or just a coincidence."

"Good question," I say. I consider it for a moment. "But in all instances, or at least in Sawyer's and mine, the vision gave us more information as time progressed. A hidden frame exposed here, an extra scene there," I say, remembering the moment I discovered Sawyer's face in the body bag.

"And in all cases, the visions appeared more frequently as the event became imminent," Sawyer says. He taps his chin. "I can't believe I'm saying this, but the way it works, it really seems like the vision gods want you to succeed."

I give a sarcastic laugh. "They're on our side, all right."

"You know what I mean."

I nod. "Yeah, I do. The vision really does give you the clues you need and the urgency to find all the answers. You just have to work at it to see them all."

As the bell rings, Trey concludes, "So maybe we should wait a few days to visit Tori, in hopes that she gets more information or some new scenes in the vision."

Sawyer and I look at each other and nod. "Let's shoot for the weekend, then," I say. "I'll let everybody know if anything changes. But I'm sure we're safe to wait until then."

Twenty-Seven

Tori gets discharged from the hospital on Tuesday to finish her lengthy recovery at home. All week I stay in touch with her, coaching her and keeping her calm despite the fact that the vision is growing more intense every day. "Even though it seems like everything is out of control, it's okay," I tell her. "You'll see more soon, and as long as you are telling me everything, we'll know when we can start to act. But right now, we just don't have enough information." I pause. "You got more information over time with your last vision, right?"

"I guess," she says. "Yeah. But this is horrible, going through it all over again. And this one is so . . . gruesome. It makes me sick to my stomach."

I rise above the urge to say she should have listened to

me last time, and instead I tell her, "Just try to stay sane. And let me know if anything changes. You can call me anytime, day or night. I mean it."

"Thanks," Tori says.

"Is your mom still being cool?"

"Yeah. No worries. She gets it now."

Friday morning Tori texts me: *It's getting worse, and I think there's something new.*

I write back: *We'd all like to come to your house tomorrow. Is that okay?*

She gives me her mom's address, and thankfully it's much closer to our house than UC is. We were going broke paying for gas.

On Saturday, Trey, Ben, Rowan, Sawyer, and I sprawl out in the Hayeses' living room, surrounding the recliner where Tori rests wearing loose-fitting sweats.

"You look fancy," I say. "No hospital gown."

"Finally," Tori says. She smiles for, like, the first time ever. "I'm so glad to be out of the hospital."

"I'll bet." I tell her about my recent time in the hospital after the crash.

"So, wait—you got hurt doing your vision thing?" Her face is troubled.

"Totally," I say. "And obviously you know Trey got

shot in the arm during the one at UC, and he was helping. He knew about the vision. He was lucky, though. He's doing physical therapy stuff now."

"Wow, that's terrible," Tori says. "I didn't realize that you guys could get hurt while doing this. That's not fair."

I glance at Sawyer, who is looking at me. "Invincible," he says decisively, and I give a reluctant half grin. I turn back to Tori. "We try not to think about that."

I officially introduce Trey and Rowan to Tori, and then I make sure Tori knows Ben since I don't know if she was at the meeting from the Gay-Straight Alliance side or the choir group side of things. Ben assures me they are well acquainted.

"Great," I say. "Let's get moving, then."

I pull out my smartphone while Ben and Sawyer set up their laptops. Tori gives us the Wi-Fi password, and within a minute we're online.

"It's like Command Central in here," Rowan says, looking around the room.

Sawyer props his computer on a small table next to Tori's chair and directs his browser to a video page. I pull out some tracing paper and a pencil that I bought from a craft store a few days ago for this purpose and set it on the floor next to Sawyer for later. We're starting to get good at this.

"Everybody ready?" Sawyer asks, looking around. We're all poised to take notes and research anything that is researchable. Sawyer starts the video. "Do you see your vision?" he asks Tori.

"Oh, yeah," Tori says. "Question is, when do I *not* see it these days?"

"Okay, good," he says. "So here's what we're going to do. I'm going to start this video from the beginning and pause immediately, which should pause your vision. Then I'm going to need you to talk us through what you're seeing little by little, scene by scene, and tell us everything. Don't leave any detail out, even if it seems unimportant. Got it?"

"Got it," Tori says.

"And then after we talk through each frozen screenshot, I'll have you do a little tracing of the scenes, if that's okay."

"Yeah, totally," Tori says. She seems very eager to redeem herself, and I'm glad. I'm actually starting to like her. She walks us through the vision.

"The first thing I see is the ship. It's all white where I'm standing, but later from a different angle I can see it's blue on the bottom."

"What's your point of view in this scene?" I ask. "Are you, you know, standing *on* the ship, or looking at it from a different spot?"

"For the first scene, I'm on the ship. Like I'm standing on a deck," Tori says. "The ship is rocking and there's a lot of spray and big swells like you'd find in the ocean. There are benches out here, and then there's a door that leads to . . . like a giant glass room, and I can see a bunch of empty seats in there. Rows of them, like in an airport terminal. Some tables, too. There's stuff strewn all around."

Ben looks up. He tilts his head, eyes narrowed, but says nothing.

"Can you see any land in this frame?" Sawyer asks.

"Not this one. Just sky. Cloudy, possibly raining, windy. Slight bit of yellow behind low clouds, like it's morning."

"Anything else? Any writing on the ship that you can see?"

"The benches have words indicating there are life vests inside. That's all I notice."

"Any people in this shot?"

"Only blurry images far inside that glass room. Nobody's sitting—if they're not on the floor, they're all in one place, crowding around."

Sawyer hands her a piece of tracing paper and the pencil, and she holds it up to the screen and quickly traces what she sees.

Tori slides the video play bar slightly to the right, narrowing her eyes and trying to get it in just the right spot. "Okay," she says. "The next scene is from farther away, like I'm not on the boat, because I can see the whole thing and a vast expanse of water behind it. There are words on the side, but I can't read them—I'm really far away, like maybe my view is from land. When this scene is in motion, there's a very sudden jolt or something. I can't really describe it, and there's no sound or anything. It's like the vision has a glitch in it. . . ." She stares at the computer and we all look at her quietly.

"Oooh," she says softly. "That's why." She looks closer at the screen. "There's something in the water, and I think the ship hits it. I never realized what that bump in the vision was until now." She touches the screen and slides her finger across it, as if we can see what she's pointing at. "There," she says. "It's like a seawall sticking out." She looks up. "It's almost invisible because the waves are so high."

"Good job, Tori," I say. "That explains a lot."

She traces this picture and Sawyer passes it around the room.

"Are the people on the floor before or after the little jolt?" I ask.

"Hmm. Before. That's weird."

I write everything down.

As Tori goes on to find the next frame, Ben studies the sketch. He looks up. "Am I allowed to ask questions or . . ."

"Please," I say. "Yes."

"Tori," he says, "I'm just curious. Have you spent

much time on the water? Sailing, fishing, swimming, anything like that?"

"No, hardly at all. I mean, my mom and I went to this little cottage once on a lake that was more like a pond, and I've spent a few hours at the beach now and then, but I'm not really a beach fan."

He smiles warmly. "So you won't be offended if I correct you?"

She laughs. "Heck no."

Ben nods and holds up her sketch. "Technically, this isn't what I'd call a ship. It's a ferry. I wondered that at first when you mentioned all the rows of seating and the glassed-in observation deck." He points to the vessel drawing. "See how stout and flat it is? Unless the computer stretched the image, I'd say this might even be a car ferry."

Sawyer looks at Ben. "Sawyer is impressed," he says, and glances at me. "Did I do that right?"

I grin. "Perfect." I turn to Ben. "Great. So, Ben, have you been on the water much?"

He scratches his head. "I have."

"What's your experience?"

"Well," he says, almost sheepishly, "my family owns a marina. And I'm also a lifeguard."

Twenty-Eight

I blink. "Seriously, Ben?"

"Yep."

"I think I'm in love right now."

"Me too," says everybody else in the room.

Ben laughs it off.

"No, I'm serious," I say. "This whole impossible feat just got a little bit easier, thanks to you. I mean, as long as it's not in an ocean somewhere." I press my lips together, forgetting that I hadn't mentioned that little caveat to Tori. If this happens in the ocean and we bail, we don't save Tori from going insane.

"My guess is it's right here in Lake Michigan," Ben says. "You can't see across it, so Lake Michigan can very easily look like an ocean, especially in a storm. There were twenty-foot waves when the remains of Superstorm Sandy pushed through here—remember that one? And that's not even the record."

"What's the record?" I ask, suddenly curious.

"Oh, heck, I don't know. Twenty-three feet, I think."

"Ben, I had no idea you were such a geek," Sawyer says with sincere admiration in his voice.

"Back off, Sawyer," Trey mutters as he types frantically on Ben's computer.

Tori moves on to the next scene, and the next, and the next, all of which offer no additional clues, though the progression of the drawings of the ferry listing and sinking lower and lower in the water is frightening.

She goes to the next. "This one I'm really curious about," she murmurs, adjusting the slide on the screen. "Right around here there are the rocks and a little glimpse of land, I think. If I can only . . . just . . ." She sticks her tongue out of the corner of her mouth as she tries to land on the scene just right.

"There," she says. She squints at the screen. "In this scene my point of view is from the other side of the ship— I mean, the ferry—as it begins to tip in the water. On the right there's a splotch of orange and I can see people on it. I think that's a lifeboat."

"Interesting," I say.

"And looking over here," she says, pointing to the

other side of the screen, "I see the top of a building." She looks closer and shakes her head. "I can't tell for sure, but I think that's what it is."

"Hang on," Sawyer says, and he rummages through his computer case. "I just remembered I snagged my mother's reading glasses back when I was going through this, and I never gave them back. This is what helped me read the stuff on the board in the classroom at UC so I could figure out which room it was."

Tori takes the glasses and puts them on, magnifying the bit of a building. "I take it back," she says after a moment. "It's the tops of two buildings. And something red over here."

"Hmm," I say. "Two buildings. The edge of a skyline, maybe? Could it be Chicago?"

"I can't tell." Tori lifts her gaze. "I'm sorry." She looks exhausted.

I check my phone clock and see we've been here for two hours. I reach out and touch her hand. "Don't be sorry. You're doing great."

She smiles. "If you say so," she says, taking a deep breath and letting it out. "Let me see what else is here."

She slides the vision forward ever so carefully. "Here's the one that makes me sick." She studies it for a moment. "The ship is half sunk, almost lying on its side, a big wave behind it. There are two lifeboats with people in the water clinging to them. And a third lifeboat that's empty, floating away, while the remaining ferry passengers fall and slide over the railing and into the water below."

She stares at the screen, and then slowly picks up a fresh sheet of tracing paper and starts another outline.

I look down at my notes, not sure what to say. It's probably better just to be silent and let her do what she needs to do.

When I look up again, Sawyer is leaning forward, eyes closed, a bead of sweat dripping down his temple. I open my mouth to ask if he's all right, but then I close it again. Because I finally realize what it is that's affecting him.

I think back to a conversation he, Trey, and I had in the school hallway about our biggest fears after Trey had said his worst nightmare was a school shooting.

"Suffocating," I remember saying mine was.

And then there was Sawyer. Who said drowning.

Twenty-Nine

Trey looks up from Ben's computer. "There are two ferry services that cross Lake Michigan," he reports. "One sails round-trip from Manitowoc, Wisconsin, to Ludington, Michigan, and the other goes between Milwaukee and Muskegon, Michigan."

Rowan, looking at her phone, chimes in triumphantly, "And the second one is white on top and blue on the bottom."

I turn to see her phone. "That's the Milwaukee one?"

"Yes." She shows it to Tori. "Is that it?"

"Wow," Tori says. "Yes, that's totally it. You guys are good."

I look at Trey. Milwaukee is a good hour-and-a-half drive from home. "So, Milwaukee. Is that within our, um, jurisdiction?"

Tori turns sharply, a look of fear in her eyes. "What do you mean? Can't you guys help me? Is there another team of you vision-solver people up there?"

Trey gives me a dirty look. "As far as we know, there aren't any other weirdos like us anywhere," he says to Tori. "So of course we'll go to Milwaukee."

And as much as I wanted to call this one off at one point, I'm glad Trey isn't going to give me a hard time about going forward. Because deep down I am fully committed, and there's no way I can let Tori deal with this on her own when the reason it's happening to her is because of me.

We pack up our things to leave and let Tori get some rest. Before I go, she asks, "Did I do all right?"

I lean down to her in the chair and give her a hug around the shoulders. "You did great," I say. "We've narrowed down one of the most important components—the *where*. Now all we need to figure out is when it happens." I groan inwardly, because the *when* has been a constant difficulty in this process.

"And how you're going to save everybody."

"Right." I haven't even thought about that part yet—the impossible part. "So if you have any ideas, feel free to pass them along." I manage a weak smile.

"I will."

"And play around some more with the vision. If you

have a DVR, you can pause, rewind, and fast-forward whenever you catch it on TV too, you know. Let me know if you find anything new." I turn to join the others outside, but then hesitate. "Where's your mother?"

Tori grins sleepily. "I told her that if she hung around during this meeting, I was going to hitch a ride with you guys to UC to recover in my dorm room."

I laugh. "I don't know how you handled it, being in the hospital with her there all the time. Did she ever leave?"

"Not often," Tori says. "I tried to get her to go to the cafeteria when I knew you were coming, but she decided she wasn't hungry." She rolls her eyes. "But," she adds, with a kinder smile, "I'm pretty much all she has. My dad died when I was a baby, so . . ." She shrugs. "I cut her some slack on the smothering."

"I'm sorry," I say.

"It's okay. I don't remember him."

"Well, I'm glad today worked out."

"Me too. Because if my mother finds out what you said about getting hurt while you're trying to save people, she'd stop everything." She emits a hollow laugh. "I guess since you and Sawyer didn't get shot, we figured you had some mystical protection or a guardian angel watching over you or something. It just doesn't seem fair other-wise."

I flash a grim smile. "No, it doesn't."

There is nothing more to say. I wave and wind my way out of her house to the car, where the others wait. I look at Ben and Trey and Ro, and I wonder how the hell I got so lucky to have people actually sign up for this.

Thirty

On Sunday, everybody's got major stuff to study for, so we decide to abandon the hive-mind approach and instead come up with ideas individually, thinking that we might even be more effective problem solvers without being steered in one group direction. We plan to meet up at Sawyer's on Monday night since he and Kate have wireless Internet.

Through it all, we hardly see my parents. They are seemingly making business work with the big truck o' balls. They've got a calendar of events stuck to the refrigerator, showing the various food truck lunches and market/food truck tie-in events, which seem to be a thing now that we're heading toward the summer months. People buy local homemade goodies, spices, and fresh produce, and then support the local food truck vendors too. And Mom and Dad have managed to book a couple of private party events in the community, which they probably wouldn't have gotten if the restaurant hadn't burned down. That last bit was Mom's look-on-the-bright-side take, actually, not mine. They're gone almost every day. And so far, since the fire, my father hasn't spent a single day in bed.

We don't quite know what to make of it, but Mom looks like she's ten years younger. So Monday morning, while I wait for Trey and Rowan for school, she happens to get up early, and I tell her that.

She smiles her beautiful smile. "Well, thanks. It helps having Dad around more," she admits, and then confides, "You know, he really likes the customer inter-action through the service window. If I'd known that would give him some spunk, I'd have had him waiting tables years ago."

I laugh. "Spunk."

"What? That word's no good anymore? I can't keep up with your lingo."

"It's totally a good word. It's cute, Mom. I'm going to start using it."

"Stop teasing me." She kisses my cheek when we hear Trey and Rowan stampeding through the living room. I grab my backpack as they drag me to the not-delivery car.

"You guys are so spunky today!" I say, loud enough for Mom to hear.

"I mean it," she calls after me.

I grin and wave.

"You're weird," Rowan says.

After school we head over to Sawyer's and arrive just as Kate is leaving for her shift at Angotti's Trattoria. She's probably the cutest person I've ever seen, with this funky short bleached-blond hair and cool piercings and gorgeous tattoos. She's kind of like a rock star to me, I guess. She's twenty-one and goes to college and has, like, a *life*, you know? Plus she took Sawyer in. So that makes her a hero, too.

I met Kate before, though I don't remember it. It was after I crashed the meatball truck into that snowplow in the Angotti's parking lot. I remember the seconds before the crash, how she was standing outside having a cigarette and our eyes locked for just a second while I screamed through the closed window at her to run.

After the crash happened, she called 911 and came running over and apparently stayed and talked to me and Trey while we waited for help to come. I don't remember that, but Trey does.

And I guess she came by the hospital to see me once, but my dad wouldn't let her in because she's an Angotti, so

Trey and Rowan hung out with her in the waiting room.

So now Trey and Rowan say hey to Kate like it's no big deal to see her again. But I get all nervous. I guess . . . I guess since I'll never talk to Sawyer's parents, I want her to like me. To have someone in Sawyer's family approve of me.

"Hey," I say. "Thanks for the bags of stuff after the fire. We all really appreciated it."

"No sweat," she says, and she gives me a hug. "Nice to see you."

I think I'm in supercrush mode with this girl. Not really, but yeah.

Sawyer introduces Ben to her, and then she's out the door, yelling behind her, "Don't eat the prosciutto or salami, I need them for a charcuterie plate!"

And that does it. Because nobody should get between a girl and her pork. I'm in love.

But there is a time for crushes, and that time is not now. And maybe not ever, if we don't figure out how to survive this sinking ferry.

Thirty-One

I bring out the sketches from Tori, and we take turns discussing our findings so far.

Trey starts. "The good news is that the sinking ferry isn't going to happen this week."

I look over from the well-stocked refrigerator, skeptical. "Because?"

"Because the ferry service hasn't started for the season yet. It starts a week from today, and there are only two ferry departure times per day. Six in the morning and twelve thirty. Since Tori sees a dim spot of light low in the sky, and the sun rises in Milwaukee ten to twenty minutes before six over the next few weeks, I deduce that this disaster happens on the early morning ferry. No idea what day, but I think this narrows down the time of day pretty nicely." Trey looks up from his notes.

"What about the Muskegon departures?" I ask, checking the fridge for snacks.

"Too late in the day to line up with the sun's position."

"Wow," I say. "Have we ever known the time of something this early on? This is huge. Good work, Trey."

Trey leans back in his chair, looking smug. "I know," he says.

I slice some chorizo and two apples and assemble a little Kate-inspired charcuterie plate of my own, adding cheese, crackers, and some walnuts I find in a cupboard, and bring it to the table for everybody to share. "What else do we have?"

My little rookie Rowan raises her hand, which is kind of adorable. "I checked the ten-day forecast and there are small chances of thunderstorms next Monday through Wednesday. That's all I can get so far. I'll keep an eye on it, though."

Ben adds, "I've done some more Lake Michigan and ferry research. There's definitely an issue with riptides in the lake, especially in relationship to breakwalls, which is what I'm guessing the ferry hits and what eventually causes it to sink. The riptides might pull down individuals in the water. Added to that, water temps are still in the forties this time of year, and anybody who doesn't make it into a lifeboat is in serious trouble."

He continues. "As for the ferry, I think it would have to hit that breakwall with quite a bit of force to damage it enough to eventually sink it. With the waves that high and visibility low, I could see it happening, but my guess is that Tori's vision isn't showing something. No little bump or glitch, as she said, would be enough to have that kind of effect."

"She said there were people on the floor of the ferry before the bump," Rowan says. "Maybe it hits more than once, and hard enough that people would be injured."

"That's what I was thinking," Ben says. "Speaking of lifeboats, the ferry has plenty of them, with more than enough room for a full-capacity voyage. But something must go wrong for one to be floating away empty. Could be the ferry's tilting—that would make it hard to exit from one side."

I glance at Sawyer, who is quiet at the stove, sautéing onions and garlic and chopping up several Roma tomatoes.

"Okay," I say. "I just have to tell you that it's such a relief not to have to do all of this myself. Thanks to all of you for putting so much work into this. We're making a lot of progress here."

"Sure," Ben says.

"You're welcome," says Rowan.

Sawyer turns around, agitation clear on his face. "Yeah, it's all really helpful, but what I'd like to know is how the hell we stop a ferry from hitting a breakwall and sinking during high seas." He rips his fingers through his hair, which he does when he's frustrated—I know that well enough by now.

"We're working on that," I say coolly. "In fact, that's what I'd like to talk about next."

He doesn't reply, so I go on. "Ben, do you have access to a boat that you'd feel comfortable driving—or sailing, I mean—in weather like that?"

Ben knits his brows. "I have access to boats, yes. But I'm not qualified to sail safely in those conditions."

"Okay, that's what I figured. No problem, it was just a thought. Next, I don't think we try to stop the ferry from hitting the breakwall. That's impossible. We can try to stop the ferry from sailing, but that kind of action never seems to work for us, right? Making strange claims of future disasters will only get us in trouble. I mean, I couldn't stop the snowplow driver from driving. We couldn't stop the shooters from attacking. So I'm assuming rather than wasting time trying to get the captain to stop the voyage, our job is to keep people from dying in the confusion that follows the impact." I pause and look at the solemn faces looking back at me. "Right? That's been our job all along. We do our best to stop people from dying." I glance at Sawyer, who is half turned, listening.

"Okay," he says. "And?"

"And so we need to be on that ferry."

The only sound is a wooden spoon scraping the bottom of a stew pot. I smell fresh basil.

After a moment, Sawyer says, "How do we save twenty or thirty people from drowning when we're on a sinking ferry?"

"By organizing the passengers and keeping them calm. Handing out life vests and helping the crew with the lifeboats. Taking charge of the situation and trying to make sure that the runaway lifeboat doesn't get detached from the ferry until it's full of people."

"And when the ship sinks?"

"We . . ." For the first time I falter. "We get into a lifeboat too."

"And then?"

"We get rescued," I say. I look down at the table, staring at the remains of the charcuterie plate, no longer hungry.

Sawyer pulls an electric hand blender from a cupboard and pulverizes the contents of his stewpan into soup while the rest of us imagine ourselves in lifeboats, crashing into breakwalls and splitting our heads open on rocks.

Or maybe that's just me.

Thirty-Two

I stay at Sawyer's when everybody else leaves.

"The soup smells delicious," I say, trying to get a peek at it over Sawyer's shoulder. "Looks great too." I wrap my arms around his waist and he pours a splash of cream into the pot. I can feel his muscles tense as he stirs.

"Almost ready," he says. He takes a clean spoon and dips it in. "Wanna test it?"

"Of course," I say. I blow on it and take a sip, closing my eyes to savor it. "This tastes like a cold fall day," I say. "I forgot it was April. *Delizioso.*"

He turns off the burner and faces me. I put my arms around his neck and he slides his around my waist, and he looks into my eyes, not smiling.

I look into his eyes, and I don't smile either. "Talk to me," I say softly. "What happened to you?"

His eyes narrow a fraction. "Nothing," he says.

I tip my head slightly. "So what's going on?"

"What do you mean?"

Our faces are inches apart.

"What is it about the water?"

He breaks his gaze. "Oh. That. It's no big deal."

I stare at him. "Come on."

He loosens his grasp on my waist and turns to look at the soup. "Okaaay," he says. "When I was ten I was kayaking on a lake with my brother. There were two guys on Sea-Doos screwing around nearby, doing stupid stunts. One of them fell off and his Sea-Doo kept going for a ways after the motor cut, and the guy wasn't wearing a life vest or anything."

Sawyer stirs and shrugs his shoulders. "He was trying to swim to the craft but he was starting to struggle, so my brother and I glided over to try to give him a hand. I took off my life vest and threw it to him while my brother tried to reach out to him. The guy was starting to freak out, and he grabbed the side of the kayak. With my brother leaning out in that direction, the kayak flipped."

"Oh no," I whisper.

"Oh yeah. So basically I wasn't prepared. I panicked. My mind went blank. I was underwater, and when I finally had enough sense to realize the kayak wasn't flipping all the way around, I tried to get out. My leg got stuck. And the Sea-Doo guy was holding on to the bottom of the kayak, so I couldn't flip it upright again."

He pulls two bowls from the cupboard. "I sucked in some water and started to black out. And you know what's so scary about starting to drown? You stop moving. You can't struggle, because you go into shock, and you have no oxygen, so you can't make noise. You just go limp."

I can hardly breathe, listening to him. "What happened?"

"My brother got me out, and I coughed and puked and started breathing on my own again. And I was fine. But I never went in any body of water over my head again."

He gets spoons for us and ladles the soup into the bowls. "I'm not a strong swimmer, either. So." He shrugs and pulls a chair out for me, and we sit and eat our soup, even though I can hardly get it down after hearing that.

"You don't have to do this, you know. You can stay back on shore and help from there."

He smiles and draws his finger over the back of my hand. "And that's why I didn't tell you this before."

"I'm just saying—"

"I know. And I'm going with you, and I don't want to talk about it anymore. I'm dealing with it, okay? And this time I'm keeping my damn life vest to myself."

Thirty-Three

Tori calls every day. Things were better for a day or two after we met at her house, she says, but as the week progresses the vision is growing stronger and more intense. By Thursday afternoon she can't watch TV because it's just the vision on a loop, and on Friday it's reflected in all the windows in her house.

"Are you sure there's nothing more?" I ask. I'm getting impatient. We really need to figure out what day this will happen.

"Nothing," Tori says. There's an edge to her voice now, and I know she's suffering. "I'm looking at everything. I promise."

"I know." I don't know what else to say. "Be sure to tell me if . . . well, you know."

"Yeah."

"And e-mail me a detailed list of what all the drowning people look like and what they're wearing."

"Got it."

We hang up. I dig the heels of my hands into my eye sockets and yell out my frustration.

Rowan comes running into the bedroom holding a dish towel. "What? Did something happen?"

"No. I'm just frustrated." I fall back on my bed, and Rowan sits next to me. She checks her phone.

"I've been watching the weather. There's still a small chance of thunderstorms pretty much every day next week, but the highest chance is Monday."

"How big is the chance on Monday?"

"Forty percent, and windy. Ten to twenty percent on the other days."

I stare at the ceiling. "My gut says this is coming soon. It's getting really bad for Tori. And that's always been an indicator that we're either doing something wrong or the tragedy is imminent. And after doing this a few times, I'm feeling relatively confident that we're getting it right except for knowing the day. So that makes me think it's imminent."

"Like Monday imminent?"

"Like Monday imminent." I close my eyes, trying to really think it through. I muse, "Do we take a chance and get tickets for Monday's six a.m. voyage? If we're wrong, we'll miss school, and that'll be really hard to explain if we have to do it again later in the week. Not to mention expensive. And since none of us is working much at the moment, the money stash is definitely dwindling."

"How much is a ticket?"

"Like eighty-five bucks."

"Sheesh."

"I know, right? Not only do we have to save people, but we also have to spend big bucks to do it. This is getting outrageous." I turn my head to look at Rowan and smile. "We could always leave you home and save some money."

"No!"

"I'm kidding. We need you. Twenty-some people to save—heck, if we had any more friends I'd recruit them, too. We need all the help we can get." I size her up. "I wonder if they have children's tickets. If you can act like a little kid, we might be able to save money by getting you one."

She snorts. "Yeah, I'll tape my boobs down and wear my Burger King crown. That'll fool 'em. They see five-foot-seven-inch-tall, hippy eleven-year-olds all the time." She leers at me. "You, on the other hand . . ."

"Did you just call me short?"

"And, apparently, boobless."

"Sawyer doesn't think so. How about Charlie? Oh,

wait, he can't even tell because he's your fake Internet boyfriend."

"Shut your face, I hate you."

"I hate you, too."

That night Sawyer comes over with a diagram he somehow found of the ferry, showing the locations of the lifeboats and all the life vests. We study the diagram and Trey takes a photo of it and e-mails it to Ben so he can look at it too.

On Friday night we check the weather forecast. It's unchanged. Ben and Sawyer come over while my parents are out at some Friday-night food truck festival.

My phone vibrates. It's Tori with her daily call.

I hold my hand up to hush everybody, and answer. "Hey, Tori, how's it going?"

"There's something new," she says, almost breathless.

"Finally," I say. "What is it?" I cover the mouthpiece and whisper, "She says there's something new."

"Two things, actually. The first thing is inside the glassed-in deck. There's, like, a banner of some sort. Like a long birthday banner, you know? I can't read what it says, not even with my mom's binoculars, but I got to thinking that maybe on the first day of the season they might put up a banner of some sort, don't you think?"

I shrug. "Yeah, sounds reasonable."

"What?" Rowan whispers.

I kick her.

"What's the other thing?" I ask Tori. Rowan pinches me, Trey slugs her, and I realize I could probably just put Tori on speakerphone to avoid this situation. "Hang on, Tori—I'm going to put you on speaker." I snarl at Rowan and press the button. "Okay, go ahead."

"The other thing is that there's a new frame added on after the frame of the two buildings in the distance. I can see more buildings—tall ones. It's definitely a skyline. So I traced it for you guys."

"Cool, that's awesome! Downtown Milwaukee is right there, I think, so that makes sense that you can see the city from the water. Do you want to scan it and send it to Sawyer's e-mail?" I give her Sawyer's e-mail address. "Send him the victim list, too, would you? Then he can print copies for us."

"You got it."

"You sound a little better today," I say.

"I'm just relieved there's more. I feel like I'm not doing a very good job of this."

"Are you kidding me? You're doing great!" I say, and the others all chime in with their praise. We need to keep her going in these last few days.

"Okay," she says, like she's embarrassed. "Let me know what the plan is when you have one."

"I will," I say. We hang up.

"What was the first thing?" Rowan asks.

"Give me a second and I'll tell you, you little pain in the butt."

"Nose," Rowan adds.

I grin reluctantly. "Nice. Anyway, she said in the glassed-in cabin there's a banner hanging, like one of those kinds you see for birthdays and graduations, you know? She can't read it, but she suggests that they might use a banner like that on opening day of a new season." The more I think about it, the more sense it makes.

"Seems reasonable," Ben says.

"Yeah, I think it make sense," Sawyer says. He pages through the sketches, and then turns to his computer when it beeps to open up the files from Tori.

I look over his shoulder. "Well, they're not the most stunning revelations we've ever had, but it's progress."

Sawyer studies his computer screen as the others come around to look.

Trey takes a look at the skyline picture. He squints and looks closer. And then he shakes his head. "Guys?" he says. "That's not Milwaukee."

Thirty-Four

We all look at Trey, and then at the skyline sketch.

"Zoom in a little, can you, Sawyer?" Trey asks.

Sawyer expands the page and zooms in.

"If she traced this correctly, and I don't know how she could possibly mess it up, this is definitely not Milwaukee." He looks at me. "In fact, I think it's the north view of Chicago."

The room explodes in questions. We all talk over each other until Trey emits a shrill whistle with his fingers.

"Knock it off, guys," he says. "I don't know how the ferry could be this close to Chicago, but it is. That's the John Hancock building, and there's the Sears Tower. Or whatever they call that building now."

"Willis," Rowan mutters, but nobody cares. It'll always be the Sears Tower.

I'm so confused. "Why is the ferry this close to Chicago? Are we sure this is the Milwaukee ferry? It shouldn't be anywhere near here. It's almost a straight shot across the lake to Muskegon."

"Tori saw the ferry's website, including a picture of the ferry," Ben says. "She said she was sure that was it. Besides, our only other option for ferries on Lake Michigan is the one that operates even farther north than Milwaukee, and it's an old nineteen-fifties schooner type—nothing like the high-speed Milwaukee ferry."

"Okay," I say, "but Milwaukee isn't just the next town north of Chicago, you know. It's like seventy miles."

"True," Trey interjects. "But Tori's sketch shows the skyline quite far away. And Chicago is on the southwest curve of the lakeshore, so it's possible to see the skyline from quite a distance."

"But I don't understand how or why the ferry would venture so far off course." I know I keep saying this, but it doesn't make sense. And I'm getting frustrated.

"Maybe there's something wrong with the ferry," Ben says. "Maybe it's not just the storm causing this. Besides, I've been thinking about the storm a lot. And if the waves were really that enormous, no captain would take a passenger vessel out to sea. I could see them taking it out in eight- or even ten-foot waves, but not much higher than that, or everybody would be yakking the whole trip. It must not be as rough as Tori made it out to be. I keep reminding myself that Tori's personal experience factors into her perspective."

I lie back on the floor and close my eyes. We've managed to come up with more questions than answers. And I'm starving. "Foooood," I groan.

Sawyer rolls over to me and rests his head on my stomach. "Yep, you're definitely hungry," he says. "And I think we can all use a break. Let's go get dinner."

"But we need to save our money for ferry tickets," I moan.

"I'm hungry too," Rowan says. "Hey, I know—we could go find Mom and Dad. They'll feed us for free. I think."

"They will," Trey says. "Well, maybe not Sawyer." He grins.

Sawyer shrugs. "I can pay. I'm not some jobless punk like you, you know." He straightens his collar. "I work with kittens." He pulls me to my feet and we all stagger to the not-delivery car and go in search of the giant balls.

While everybody chatters around me, I realize the thing that's so unsettling about the ferry within sight distance of Chicago is that it would take quite a long time for it to travel that far. And if Tori's spot of potential light low in the sky is actually the sun, I need to know how low in the sky it really is. And if it's possible for it to still be "low in the sky" if it takes a while to get from Milwaukee to the location in the vision.

Tori didn't draw the possible sun on the sketch. I text her. *What would you guess is the angle of that spot of yellow to the Earth?*

Sawyer peeks at what I'm doing. He nods. "Yeah, I was wondering the same thing."

Tori replies: *I was told there would be no math.*

"Oh, look," I say. "Tori's being funny for the first time in her life. She must be feeling better."

"I bet it's because we're figuring things out."

We wait, and in a few minutes she has an answer. *Around thirty degrees, I guess.*

I glance at Sawyer as Trey pulls into the parking lot for the Friday-night food truck festival. "You up for a little early morning research at North Avenue Beach tomorrow?"

"I don't start work until one," he says.

"Cool. I can probably get the car. I'll pick you up at five?"

"Oof, that's early. Yeah, sounds good. It'll be cold out there by the water."

"We can snuggle," I say. "I'll bring a blanket."

He wraps his arms around me and kisses the side of my head. "I like it. We can do more sexy time."

"You don't *do* sexy time. You have it."

"Yes, yes, I do," he says.

"Please stop now," Rowan remarks. "Gross. It's time to eat some juicy balls."

"Dot-com," I add. Hey, it's good to mix things up a little.

Thirty-Five

"There's probably a math problem that will tell us the answer here," Sawyer says. We snuggle together under a blanket on the beach facing the water, looking toward Michigan even though we can't see it, and watch the sunrise.

"Yeah, but any math problem that relies on the rotation of the Earth makes my head explode," I say. "Besides, this is more fun."

Sawyer rolls onto his side, facing me, and rests his hand on my stomach, his fingers tracing the stitching on my pullover. He nuzzles my neck. My skin tingles. I close my eyes and suck in a breath. My brain argues with my body, but my body wins. I turn toward Sawyer and slip my arm under his head, and my lips find his.

His hand travels to the small of my back and pulls me close, our legs entwining. In all our layers of clothes and blanket, we kiss, gently, softly. We touch our foreheads together and exist, for a moment, only in each other's eyes. I pull the blanket over our heads and we lie there, just kissing and touching and being close and safe and free of all the stress. I would lie like this forever if I could.

"I love you," I whisper.

"Yes, yes, you do." Sawyer grins and kisses me, and I grin too and our teeth click together. "Ow," he says, laughing.

The spell is broken. The brain wins round two. I pull the blanket off our faces and check the sun. Not quite there.

We wait and watch, mostly in silence amid gentle, somewhat absentminded caresses, cool fingers on bare skin, as the Earth turns us. As we focus on the task we're here to do, my mind moves to logistics. I think we're both trying to visualize this rescue and how it has to happen.

"We just need to put our life vests on first," I say at one point. "That's what's going to keep us alive."

"I know," Sawyer says.

"I wasn't telling you. I was just talking out loud."

He turns his face toward mine with the hint of a smile. "Oh."

Later, he says randomly, "Rope." He sits up. "Are you free tomorrow afternoon?"

"Duh." I shield my eyes from the sun with my hand. It's getting close to the thirty-degree-angle mark.

He pulls out his phone and sends a few text messages, then settles back down.

I pull out my protractor, scoot out from under the blanket, and set the tool on its edge on a mostly smooth portion of sand that looks like it's pretty level. Then I lie on my stomach and put my face in the sand next to it. I use a thin stick to project the thirty-degree line and wait.

"It's close. What time is it?"

Sawyer checks. "Eight fifteen."

I dig a little hole in the sand for my face, to make sure my eye is lined up with the protractor. My eyes water. "Should have brought sunglasses," I mutter.

"What exactly are you doing?" Sawyer asks. I can hear the amusement in his voice.

"I don't know! I'm just trying to think logically." I sit up and wipe the sand from my cheek. "The ferry leaves at six. It is now eight fifteen and the sun is in the position where Tori believes it to be behind the clouds. The question is, could the ferry get this far in two hours and fifteen minutes? I say absolutely yes, but only if it intended to, and at a reasonably high speed."

"But that is not the normal intent of this ferry."

"Correct. So what would have to happen to make the pilot of the ferry go so off course?"

We contemplate.

"All I can think of is the mafia," Sawyer says, half joking.

"Maybe it's hijacked. It can go wicked fast, you know. Or," I say, "I know—maybe there's a different vessel in trouble, and because the ferry can carry so many passengers, and because it's fast, the Coast Guard calls them to assist."

Sawyer drums his fingers on his thigh, considering. "That actually sounds plausible. Remember when that plane landed in the Hudson River in New York? Didn't the ferries come to help pick up people?"

"I don't know. But," I say, thinking of something new, "if the weather is too windy and the lake is choppy, a helicopter wouldn't be useful. Plus they can only rescue one person at a time."

We both think about it.

"And then," Sawyer says, "maybe in the act of saving the people on the other vessel and riding the crazy waves, the ferry smashes against a breakwall. It takes on water fast, plus the waves are getting higher and water rushes in over the sides, too, and in a matter of minutes, it's the *Titanic*."

"Man, that would suck for those people from the other shipwreck to be rescued and then immediately be in another one. Two shipwrecks in a matter of hours? Now that's a bad day."

"But the irony makes it feel right, doesn't it? I mean, unbelievably tragic shit like that happens all the time."

I stare out over Lake Michigan, which is deceptively calm this morning, with light waves washing ashore. I check the weather on my phone. The chance of thunderstorms has increased to 50 percent on Monday, and decreased to between 0 and 10 percent the rest of the week.

"Sawyer," I say, "based on the weather forecast and the banner Tori saw, I'm convinced this is happening on Monday. I think we should plan on being on that ferry in Milwaukee at six a.m."

Thirty-Six

We do a quick conference call on the way home from the beach. I explain my reasons for believing the ferry disaster is happening on Monday, and after a short discussion, everybody agrees. Ben, who has a credit card, buys five tickets for Monday at six a.m. We plan to pick up Ben at four (groan) and drive up to Milwaukee together.

Saturday night, after Sawyer gets done playing with kittens at the Humane Society, he and I meet up at Tori's to see how she's doing.

Her mom lets us in. "She's a wreck," Mrs. Hayes says fretfully. "Are you sure this will go away?"

"If we have all the clues right and we manage to save some people, it will go away." I'm still a little wary of her.

I don't need her obstructing things now. But she doesn't argue and she stays out of our way.

Tori is sitting in the same recliner as last time we were here. Her eyes are closed. "I'm awake," she says. "Just resting. Trying to get away from it for a bit." The vision must be playing out everywhere.

"How has it been?" I ask.

"A little better starting this morning."

Sawyer and I exchange a glance. Did we do something right today by deciding to buy tickets? Sure seems that way.

"Is there anything new?"

"No."

I take in a deep breath and let it out slowly. "We bought our tickets for Monday."

Tori nods slowly. "That makes sense to me." She opens her eyes. "I wish this didn't have to happen at all, but since it does, the sooner the better."

"We're going to need to be in touch with you," I say. "Call or text my phone if anything changes. I want you to watch the vision Monday morning starting at six, okay? Watch it like crazy, and send me a text now and then even if nothing's changing."

"I will, Jules. I promise."

"Okay." I look at Sawyer and he nods. I squeeze Tori's hand. "We're going to let you rest now. I'll call you if anything changes, but plan on this happening Monday morning."

"Thanks," she says. "And please be safe. I'd rather deal with this than have any of you get hurt. I mean it."

"We'll be fine," Sawyer says. But he kind of looks like he's going to hurl.

Mrs. Hayes walks us out and thanks us again.

On the ride home, I realize how exhausted I am from getting up early and thinking hard about this all day. Sawyer's tired too. I drop him off at Kate's, drive home, and go straight to bed.

Ben and Sawyer show up shortly after Mom and Dad go to mass on Sunday morning. Ben comes into the house carrying two thick garment bags. Sawyer arrives with duffel bags.

"Are you guys moving in?" Rowan asks with a grin.

Ben smiles. "Got a little surprise," he says. He opens the first garment bag and pulls out four wet suits. He eyeballs Sawyer and picks one, then does the same for Trey. "Try these on. They'll keep us warm if we end up in the water. Not commando, please—they're rentals. Here are instructions on the best way to get them on." He hands each of them a half sheet of paper. "Main thing is to take your time. They should fit tightly. Don't dig your fingernails in."

Sawyer looks at the wet suit like it might bite him. Trey takes both suits and drags Sawyer along with him, shoving him into the bathroom, and then continues to his bedroom.

"I can't wait to see your package in that suit," I call out.

"Thanks!" Trey answers.

"Not you!"

"Jules," Rowan says, disgusted.

"What? Might as well point out the obvious elephant in the room instead of stare and say nothing."

"I'm not quite *that* big," comes Sawyer's muffled response through the bathroom door.

Rowan rolls her eyes and turns to Ben. "Won't we look weird wearing them on the ferry?" Rowan asks.

"You can wear clothes over it. No one will even notice. These are top-of-the-line, superflexible, and you'll have complete range of motion."

"You're brilliant, Ben," I say. "How did you get these?"

"We rent them out at the marina. I woke up this morning and couldn't believe I hadn't thought of snagging some before. My parents are out of the country, so I didn't even need an excuse to grab a bunch of sizes I thought would fit." He unzips the other garment bag and pulls out a few more, then takes a good look at us and hands them over. "Let me know if you need a different size," he says, loud enough for the guys to hear too.

It takes forever to get them on. Once we have the right sizes figured out, we're exhausted. Ben then hauls out some green life vests that are so petite they look like they couldn't possibly hold us up in the water, but he assures us they are some of the best around. We practice getting into them, and then we have to take everything off again. We make plans to wear our wet suits from the time we get up tomorrow morning so we don't have to mess with them on the ferry.

Once we're back into regular clothes, Sawyer gives us an evil grin and holds up one of the duffel bags. "My turn," he says. "Get in the car."

Thirty-Seven

"Rock climbing?" I ask.

Sawyer leads the way into the gym. "It's a class. We're taking it."

"This is like seventh-grade PE all over again, when everybody called me gay," Trey grumbles.

"Me too," Ben says glumly.

"Clearly their taunts had no effect on either of you," Rowan says.

"I'm basically gay in defiance," Trey says. "Rowan, can you write me an excuse to get me out of this?"

"Because you're gay?"

"No, loser, because I *got shot* last month. Sheesh." He rubs his shoulder.

"Yeah, I thought about that," Sawyer says. "Just take it easy and don't overdo it, Trey."

Trey flashes a triumphant look.

"You're such a rebel." Ben slips his arm over Trey's shoulders and turns to Sawyer. "Now explain this. What are we doing? Is this the traditional day-before-disaster team-building event or something? Please tell me I don't have to do a trust fall. Because the last time I did a trust fall was in seventh-grade PE. Just saying."

"Yeah, what is this?" Rowan asks. "I don't want to mess up my hair, because I have to say good-bye forever to Charlie tonight in case I whiff."

"Oh my God," I mutter. "You and your hair."

"Nobody's going to whiff," Sawyer says. "We're invincible."

I shiver when he says it.

"We're here to learn the basics, mainly because I think rope might be our friend tomorrow. So we're going to learn how to tie knots and effectively throw ropes for rescue and use the belay apparatus just in case, and we're going to do a little practice climbing on the wall, too."

We learn the ropes (har har) of rock climbing for a couple of hours. We decide not to do too much because we don't want to be sore tomorrow, but the instructor shows us a lot of useful things that might come in handy in rescuing people from a sinking ferry.

The rest of the day we wander around our neighborhood and the elementary school playground, looking like your typical hoodlums, talking through our plan, enjoying the sunshine, and watching the clouds build in the west. "There's our storm," Rowan says. "It's causing flight delays in Minneapolis right now. Tomorrow morning's forecast for Milwaukee is now seventy percent chance of thunderstorms, occasionally heavy with gusty winds."

And while that scares me, it also reassures me, and pretty much guarantees that we're doing things right.

I sit on the swings and talk to Tori for a bit. "She's hanging in there," I report to the others after I hang up. "The vision has calmed down a little." I look at my shoes, dusty from the playground. "I think this is the most prepared we've ever been."

We go over the list of victims—now sitting at twenty-seven, according to Tori. We note what they're wearing and discuss our plan to find them in advance and split them up so we each have five or six to monitor.

When it starts to get dark and our stomachs are growling, we reluctantly part. Sawyer goes to Kate's, Ben drives back to UC, and we three Demarcos head inside our house, lured by the smells of something delicious cooking in the kitchen and the pleasant faces of two seemingly normal parents who are happy to see us and enjoying life. Bizarre.

All I know is that if anything happens to us now . . . it'll pretty much wreck everything.

Thirty-Eight

We all sleep terribly for about five hours, and are extra quiet getting ready so our parents don't wake up. Which they never do. Their body clocks are permanently on restaurant time, which means late to bed, late to rise. I see their faces before school so rarely I can count the number of times on one hand.

Shortly after three, we're off. Clad in wet suits and sweats, each of us carrying a duffel bag containing a life vest and rope, we are a glaringly obvious group of kids who are clearly skipping school and running away from home. Rowan, who can do Mom's voice best, remembers to call the absentee hotline and report us all absent so Mom and Dad don't get a call later.

We pick up Sawyer first, who is waiting at the

entrance of Kate's apartment building. He holds my hand in the backseat, not saying much, his face strained. By four, the rain has started. We reach the UC campus and Ben hops into the backseat next to me. He's wearing contacts today, not his usual glasses. He gives my arm a friendly squeeze and whispers, "We got this, kid," for which I am more grateful than I expect to be. The journey continues.

The wind picks up, blowing unidentifiable bits of floaty garbage across the highway, and the rain is steady. Occasional lightning streaks across the sky. There's not much traffic heading out of Chicago at four in the morning, and we make great time, reaching the ferry terminal before five thirty. Trey parks the car and we sit for a moment, listening to the rain on the car's roof and spraying the windows.

"I have to pee," Rowan says. It breaks the mood, and I'm glad she's here.

"Good luck with that," Trey says.

It might be our first mistake, putting these wet suits on at home. "I blame Ben," I say.

"Yeah," he says. "I forgot about that part. It's not as easy to pee in the suits if you're not actually in the lake."

I look at him. "Are you saying these suits have been peed in by strangers?"

"I'd say that's pretty likely."

I close my eyes as the giant wave of grossness washes over me.

"Why do you think I told you not to go commando?"

There is silence.

"We clean them, though, obviously," Ben adds.

I hold up a hand to him. "Okay, no. Let's pretend we never had this conversation." I take in a resigned breath and loop my fingers around my duffel bag. "Come on, guys. Let's do this. Are you ready?"

The murmur of agreement is soft but resolute. We have a plan.

Ben hands over our tickets and we board. The ferry is bigger than I pictured, and I imagine how monstrous and strange it'll look tipped on its side. I grip my duffel bag tighter.

I catch a glimpse of the vehicles driving onto the ferry and wince, wishing I could tell everyone to leave their cars on land. And themselves. One good thing about the weather this morning is that it's probably keeping people from using the ferry. But there are still plenty of passengers boarding.

We take a tour of our surroundings. There's a private room for first-class passengers. I peek through the open doorway, and hastily back out when a guy in a suit gives me a cool stare.

And there's the banner. WELCOME TO OUR 13TH SEASON, it reads.

"Lucky thirteen," Rowan remarks.

Glass doors and stairways lead to multiple open decks, which would be great on a sunny summer day, but everyone stays inside the glassed-in area today. There's a snack bar, where passengers line up to get coffee and breakfast. We seek out the location of the lifeboats and flotation devices, and assign a lifeboat to each of us to man—if things work out to enable us to man them. That's the thing. Who knows how this goes down? Who knows how hard that bump is when the ferry hits the wall? And what else happens that we don't know about? I know there's got to be something that puts people on the floor before the jolt.

Once we feel comfortable with the layout, we find a spot with a table by the window and sit around it, keeping our duffel bags close by.

"This feels weird," Trey mutters. He drums his knuckles on the table. "It's really different compared to the other ones."

I nod. "The others were high tension, counting down to an exact time, and then over in seconds. This one's going to feel like it's going in slow motion, I think."

Rowan and Sawyer study the list of victim descriptions and look around for matches. Ben pulls his list out too. "This could be heartbreaking if we let it be," he says. I follow his line of sight to a family with a baby coming on board.

And I know what he means. I'm glad he said it, because that means he's thinking the way you have to think when you are doing a job like this.

I text Tori, letting her know our status, and she replies immediately, saying things are getting crazy strong. As the ferry's engines rev and we begin to pull away, I can only hope the crazy strong vision is because it's imminent, and not because we're doing something wrong.

"We're moving," I say. I look around at the people who stand by the windows, watching us leave land, and everything inside me wants to scream, "Go back!"

Trey fidgets. After a moment he stands up. "I'm going outside to look for more life vests. I can't stand sitting here."

And I watch the time, knowing there's only so far we can go before the pilot—or whoever is sailing this thing—will take a sharp turn south.

Thirty-Nine

The minutes tick away, and soon we are past the pier and on the open lake. The ferry speeds up and flies over the choppy water. And damn, it's rough. People take their seats and try to keep their coffee from spilling. A few stumble to the bathrooms, and I see somebody puking into a white barf bag. I look at Sawyer, who is gripping the table with one hand and staring at his victim list with the other. He looks ill.

"You okay?" I ask.

"Yeah. Trying not to be sick. I'm not good with spinning rides at theme parks, either."

I smile and reach into my bag. "You'll do better if you look out the window rather than at the paper." I pull a box of Dramamine out and give him a dose, along with a small bottle of water. "Try this."

He downs the pills and looks out the window through half-slit eyes.

Rowan leans over, her sweet brown eyes troubled. "I only see one person who vaguely matches any of the descriptions of the victims," she says quietly. "That guy over there."

"We might need to move around a little to find everyone. And there's the first-class cabin—there could be people in there who we can't see."

"Some of the descriptions are pretty general," Sawyer says. He keeps his eyes on the horizon.

I check my phone for what must be the twentieth time, and then glance around, nervous. "We should be turning soon," I mutter. I stand up to see if I can keep my balance. The rocking is getting more and more pronounced, and hardly anybody is trying to walk around.

Ben looks at me, concern in his eyes. "Where's Trey?"

"I was just wondering that." And then I see him pushing open the door to come inside the cabin. The wind catches the door and he has to pull it closed. His hair is everywhere, and he looks damp, but not soaked. He makes his way over to our table like a drunk, staggering from side to side trying to stay level.

"Jesus futhermucker," he says under his breath, grabbing the table and swinging heavily into a chair. "There. Well, that was an adventure." He catches his breath and grins at Ben, who is looking rather stern.

"What's the status?" Trey asks.

"Rowan thinks she found one person on the list," I say. "That guy with the tie." Everybody turns, and I feel like we're in an episode of *Scooby-Doo*. "Don't all look at once, gosh." I duck when the guy looks at us and frowns.

"I don't know anymore," Rowan says. "He's a maybe."

"That's it?" Trey says.

"So far," she says.

I look at the time. It's been thirty minutes, and according to my compass app, we're still heading northeast.

"Hey, Sawyer?" I ask.

"Yeah, baby." He peels his eyes from the horizon and looks at me.

"Why aren't we turning?"

"I don't know."

I catch Trey's eye, and I don't have to say anything for him to know I'm getting anxious. "We should be turning," I say again.

Rowan bites her lip and stands up. "I need a new angle," she says. She walks forward like she's climbing a hill, and then suddenly lurches the rest of the way across the expanse of the ferry, grabbing the backs of chairs and whatever else she can reach. She disappears around a corner. I stare out the window at the rolling waves and whitecaps gnashing at the ferry. The sky gets noticeably lighter over the next few minutes. We have outrun the storm.

By the time Rowan returns with only one more possible match, it's six forty-five. The waves are growing calmer, and we are heading in the opposite direction of where the ferry sinks. There's no way we could get there now.

Everybody realizes it, but nobody says it. When Tori texts me, saying things are getting worse, I know it's not because the tragedy is imminent.

Another ten agonizing minutes pass in silence.

"It's not today," I say finally. I close my eyes and let out a sigh, and then drop my head into my folded arms on the table, thinking of all the problems I just triggered by getting the day wrong. A missed school day, which we'll have to do again once we figure out the right day. Another ticket home. And then another ferry ticket on the *right* day, if we can even figure out when that is . . . and then there's the whole emotional mess of getting psyched up for this all over again.

"Jules is not impressed," I say into my sweatshirt sleeves. "Not impressed at all."

Forty

Everybody tries to tell me it's not my fault, and they remind me they agreed with my assessment, but I feel terrible about it. I don't even have any money on me to buy a ticket home—I figured I'd just lose it anyway in the ferry disaster.

Ben has his wallet, though, already zipped up tight with his cell phone in the waterproof pocket of his life vest inside his duffel bag, and he says he has enough money in his bank account to cover everybody's tickets as long as we can pay him back this week.

The problem is, it's really difficult to get a decent cell phone signal out in the middle of Lake Michigan, and every time he tries to buy tickets for the ten fifteen ferry back to Milwaukee, he gets the gray wheel of death. Finally he gives up.

"We'll have to buy them at the terminal," he says.

When we get to the terminal in Muskegon, it's nine thirty local time, and once we disembark, there's a line for tickets.

Finally it's our turn.

"Two seats left," the woman says. "I can't give you five."

We look at each other, mildly panicked, unsure what to do.

"I've got five seats available on the four forty-five ferry," the woman says.

"Shall we take the two and then three of us go later?" Rowan asks.

"No," Trey says. "We only have one car in Milwaukee, so whoever would take this ferry would just be stuck in Milwaukee waiting for the rest of us. Let's all take the four forty-five."

"Yeah, good thinking," I say, relieved. "We'll just have to call Mom and tell her we're doing stuff after school today."

Ben buys the tickets, and then we go into the restrooms to peel off our wet suits and redress in our sweats. I wish I'd brought other clothes, but that would have been senseless if things had gone the way I expected.

We all find bench seats in the terminal to curl up in

and take naps, which should come easily after the night and morning we had, but I can't sleep. I lie there, eyes open, wondering where I went wrong. I text a bit with Tori, who is starting to lose it. She can't see her phone anymore to text, so her mother is doing it for her. After a few more messages, I step outside the terminal to call her.

Her mom answers and hands the phone to Tori.

"How bad is it?" I ask. "Tell me everything."

"Jules," she says softly, "it's so bad now that I can feel the water rising up around me."

Whoa. When we hang up, I check the weather forecast, and tomorrow looks to be a beautiful day. "Maybe it's a freak storm over the lake," I mumble to myself. "Or maybe I shouldn't put so much stupid faith in spring weather forecasts, since they're wrong half the time anyway."

By afternoon everyone's awake and starving, and nothing in the terminal looks appetizing. We decide to explore outside, and find a cool little hot dog shop nearby for a cheap lunch. Apparently we look old enough, or confident enough, not to be questioned about being there on a school day.

While we eat, we can hear thunder rolling in the distance. Sawyer takes a look out the window at the darkening skies and decides against finishing his second dog in case the ride to Milwaukee is rough.

Fat drops of rain hit the ground as we walk back to the

terminal. We go over everything we know for the thousandth time, trying to figure out where we went wrong and what obvious clue we're missing. I wish I could see the vision just a few times. It's so frustrating having to rely on Tori to look for all the clues. What if she's the one who is missing something? What if she doesn't know what to look for? What if she misinterpreted something? All I know is that we're either doing something very, very wrong, or this thing is happening tomorrow, or maybe the next day. Yet . . . we can't keep riding this ferry forever, trying to figure it out.

Rowan calls Mom to let her know we'll be home late tonight. And finally the afternoon ferry pulls in. We watch the stream of passengers get off, and then wearily we board the ferry for the two-and-a-half-hour ride to Milwaukee.

Sawyer takes his Dramamine before he feels sick this time, which should help him. He holds me close and I manage to fall asleep to the sound of driving rain hitting the windows. The rocking is almost soothing, since I know Sawyer won't let me fall. I drift into a hard nap and dream about Tori sinking under murky waves.

When I hear Rowan saying my name, and I feel her tugging at my arm, I have to struggle to wake up, and I can't remember where I am.

"Jules!" she says. And soon Sawyer is joining in.

I open my eyes and stare at the strange surroundings for a moment before I remember. "What's up?" I say. My voice sounds like it's far away. I sit up a little and see enormous waves rolling around the ferry, lightning streaking through the sky, and nervous passengers staring out the windows.

Everybody's looking at me. "What?" I say again. I look at Sawyer. "Are you sick?"

"Jules," Trey says, "did you hear the announcement?"

"What?"

"The pilot just came on the loudspeaker. He said there are tornado warnings in Milwaukee, and marine warnings for waterspouts all along the Wisconsin shoreline."

"Waterspouts?" I blink. "Okay. How far away are we?"

"We're an hour from Milwaukee and the storm supercell is heading straight toward us, so the pilot says we're being diverted to a different port and buses will take everybody back to Milwaukee." His face is intense. "We're being diverted to Chicago, Jules. We're turning south right now, and we're heading for Chicago."

Forty-One

At first I can't comprehend what Trey is saying. The ferry lurches and rolls as the waves get bigger. "But the sun won't be right if it happens now," I say.

"I know, but maybe the ferry leaves from Chicago tomorrow morning," he says.

"Yeah," Sawyer says, sitting up. "That would put the ferry in the right place!"

"Hey, guys?" Ben says.

I close my eyes to concentrate. "But . . . but the passengers will still show up at the Milwaukee terminal—how would any of them know—"

"Because they can send an e-mail to everybody who pre-bought tickets to let them know of the change due to the weather," Trey says.

"Guys?" Ben says again.

I am still not sold. "Why wouldn't they just sail the ferry back to Milwaukee tonight after the storms pass?"

"*Guys,*" Rowan says this time.

We all look at her and Ben.

"What?" Trey says impatiently.

Rowan looks sidelong across the ferry and points her head in the direction she wants us to look. "There's the guy who is on the list. The one who rode with us this morning."

I narrow my eyes. "I thought you weren't sure."

"We weren't sure," Ben says, "until now, when we also spotted that girl sitting at ten o'clock to you, Jules." He shows me the victim list and points. "This girl," he says, "is her."

"And," Rowan continues, "I see two more. No, make that three."

I follow her gaze as I watch a woman lurch toward the bathroom. "No," I say, and then I grab the list and compare Tori's descriptions with the people Ben and Rowan are pointing out. A girl about thirteen with blond hair and a polka-dot headband. A black-haired woman in a red skirt and jacket. An older couple wearing matching sweatshirts from the Wisconsin Dells.

"Shit," Sawyer says in a low voice as he reads the list over my shoulder. "There's another one."

"But . . . the sun is wrong," I say weakly.

"Or maybe that light behind the clouds wasn't the sun," Trey says.

"Or . . ." My mind flies everywhere, combing over all the conversations I've ever had with Tori. "Or maybe Tori's sunrise is actually . . . a sun*set*?" I feel my throat close. "What time is it?" I scrounge around for my phone, finally remembering that I put it in my duffel bag. I grab it and check the time. It flips between six thirty-two and five thirty-two, depending on whether my phone is picking up a signal from the east side or the west side of the lake.

I see five new text messages from Tori, and I flip through them. *The water,* she says, again and again. *The water. It's rising. It's pouring into my mouth. It's flowing from my eyeballs. I can't breathe.*

While everybody waits for me to say something profound, I sit with my eyes closed, feeling sick and totally inadequate to lead this task. Trying to organize my crazy thoughts. Trying to figure out what to do first. Trying not to hyperventilate.

I suck in a deep breath, blow it out, and open my eyes. "Okay, guys." My voice shakes a little, which pisses me off.

I sit up straighter and start again, stronger. "Okay. This is happening. First, we take turns getting our wet suits back on without drawing attention to ourselves, which could be difficult with all the rocking and the pukers waiting for your stall. Rowan and Sawyer, you first, and when you get back, tackle the rest of the victim list."

Trey gives me the tiniest smile of encouragement, and I know he's proud of me.

"Ben, how are you with math?"

"Decent," he says.

"Good. See if you can figure out how fast we're going and how far we are from the disaster point so we can have a clue how much time we have."

"Got it." He pulls his phone out and starts working.

"Trey," I say.

"Yes?"

I blow out a breath. "First, don't die."

"Okay."

Ben looks up at us for a second, presses his lips together, and goes back to work.

"Second, I need you to use your amazing charm to try to talk to the pilot, or at least one of the crew, and try to tell them to steer clear of the low rock walls—"

Trey closes his eyes, a pained expression on his face.

"What?" I say.

"They won't listen, Jules. But I will try. I'll give it everything I've got."

"That's all I'm asking," I say. "Maybe you can convince them to ask passengers to put their life vests on." My throat hurts, and I know he's right—they won't listen to a teenager.

"I get it," Trey says. "I do. We have to try everything."

"Thanks."

Trey stands up carefully and aims for the nearest chair to grab on to, and he's on his way.

I sniff hard and pick up the victim list, staring blindly at it, thinking about the blond girl with the polka-dot headband.

I look out the rear starboard side of the ferry toward Milwaukee and see a gorgeous family of four waterspouts spinning like dust devils, connecting lake and sky.

Forty-Two

I point the waterspouts out to Ben as others on the ferry notice too.

"They're amazing," Ben says. "I've never seen one before."

I nod. I can't stop watching.

"You're doing great, Jules," he says. "I mean it."

I look at him, at the sincerity in his eyes, and I can see why Trey has fallen so hard for this guy. "Thanks. Thanks for helping us."

"How could I not?" comes his simple reply. "My life was saved in that music room. There's got to be a reason for that. I figure this is it." He looks at me. "What I can't figure out is *your* dedication to this phenomenon. You've never been saved from anything, yet you feel such a strong need to rescue others."

I shrug. It's too much to explain right now. As I spot Rowan making her way back to the table with her duffel bag, Ben turns back to his phone and says, "We've got about forty minutes."

I set the stopwatch on my phone. "Okay. Thanks. You change into your wet suit when Sawyer's back." I grab my bag and stagger toward the bathroom, pointing Rowan's attention in the direction of the waterspouts. And I'm amazed there is so much beauty in this carnivorous lake, and on this doomed ferry.

It takes forever to get my wet suit on. I bang against the sides of the stall and once nearly step into the toilet as I try to glide my second skin on without puncturing it with my fingernails. I grab on to the toilet paper holder and the purse hooks more than once as the ferry pitches from side to side, and slam against the stall wall, scaring the person next to me, before finally getting my wet suit on. Quickly I slip my life vest on and clip it into place like Ben suggested, and pull my sweatshirt over top. The vest is slight enough to fit underneath, I can move really well, and it'll save time later. I pull up my sweatpants, then replace my shoes and head back to the table.

Ben has already changed and beat me back to home base, and Sawyer's back too. Only Trey is missing.

"He's changing now," Ben says.

"Does everybody have their vests on?" I ask, though it's slightly obvious if you're looking in the right place.

"Yes," they all report.

"Timers set?"

Again, the answer is yes.

"Have we located all the victims?"

"All but five," Rowan says, "and they're all described as men or women wearing suits. So we figured they're in the first-class cabin."

"That makes sense," I say. "And since they're all grouped in one place, who wants to be in charge of them?"

"I will," Rowan says. "I've got their descriptions memorized. I'm going to accidentally go in there right now just to get a look."

She goes, and Trey returns from the bathroom with a bit of a bulge around his waist.

"Life vest?" I ask.

He nods.

"What did they say?"

He smiles ruefully. "Pretty much what you'd expect. I spoke to an officer of some sort, who assured me that the pilot has sailed these waters many times. He thanked me for putting my trust in the crew on this 'unusual' voyage."

I nod. "At least we tried. Thank you."

We divide up the rest of the victims based on where they're sitting, and assign a person to be on the lookout for them. It's the best plan we can think of, though there's sure to be chaos. Then we figure out where we're each going to get life vests from, and determine that the outside deck is the best place since no one will be out there to trample us until they start exiting to the lifeboats. And then we go over our final plan and make sure everybody knows what to do once the ferry makes contact with the breakwall.

Our valuables are put away in our waterproof vest pockets. Our duffel bags are unzipped so we can grab ropes quickly if necessary. We are as ready as we can be. And now all we can do is wait.

Ben stands and walks over to the window, better on his feet in these conditions than the rest of us. He looks for a moment and then beckons me to join him. Either the waves are not as bad now, or I'm getting better at this.

He points to the shore, where I can see buildings in the distance. "We're passing Waukegan. On a clear day you can see Chicago from here. Obviously that isn't today. But we're getting close. North Chicago is coming fast." He points at the sky. "See how it's clearing in this direction?"

I look, and there's the little spot of yellow behind thin clouds. It's not down quite far enough to match Tori's description of thirty degrees, but I'm sure now that this is Tori's sunrise—except it's a sunset. I'm disgusted with myself for not even considering it. She was just so sure. . . . I shake the negative thoughts from my head. No time to dwell on that now.

We watch the land grow closer. My phone vibrates from within the waterproof pocket of my life vest. I'm sure it's Tori. I hide my front from the passengers and reach in to get it.

SCENE CHANGE—now only 23 dead. You're doing something right! Also, NEW SCENE—big jolt right before smaller bump, then shot of ferry instrument panel covered with blood! Be careful!

Forty-Three

I text back in a frenzy, willing my fingers to hit the right buttons as we rock and churn: *Is there a clock on the instrument panel??*

And then I wait, frozen, begging her to narrow down the time of this imminent disaster. I show Ben, and he heads back to our table to tell the others about the big jolt.

Finally Tori replies: *6:38!!*

I look at the time. It's 6:35. "Shit," I mutter. And then something inside me explodes and kicks me into gear. I stagger over to the others. "Three minutes, guys. The big jolt is at six thirty-eight."

There's a split second when everyone takes in the news.

Then Ben calls 911, giving them the approximate

location as if we've already hit. Smart move. Every minute counts—especially when it comes to drowning.

"We should warn people to brace themselves," Sawyer says. "Most won't listen, but some might."

"Good," I say. "Yes. And remember—stay braced for two jolts. Then outside for life jackets, victims, lifeboats, rope. Everybody have their victim descriptions in mind?"

At 6:37, with no additional news, I shove my phone back into my waterproof pocket, seal it, and leave it there. We wait an agonizing thirty seconds, situating ourselves behind our table. Then Sawyer stands up and yells, "Brace yourselves! Everybody! Hang on!"

People turn to look at him, some in fear, others in annoyance.

"Hang on!" I echo, and so do the others. I grab the table, make sure Rowan is in a good spot. "I love you guys," I say. "See you on the other side of this one!"

Sawyer leans over and kisses me hard on the lips. "I love you."

"I love you, too," I whisper.

And then we hit.

Forty-Four

Five things that should never be airborne on a ferry:
1. A cat in a carrier
2. Golf clubs
3. Steaming-hot coffee
4. Any kind of coffee, really
5. Humans

The first jolt is a doozy, let me tell you. Not like the "run into a brick wall and stop" kind, but the "holy hell, that'll slow down a fast-moving ferry in a hurry" kind. My ribs slam into the table edge, which takes my breath away. Trey ends up on the floor, but he signals he's okay.

Everyone else in the ferry who wasn't bracing or

wedged behind a table is now on the floor. There's a second of weird silence, and I realize the engines have shut down, and then the cries of pain and the shouts begin, along with a muted chorus of honking horns and car alarms coming from belowdecks. I look out the window and see nothing but water, and a ways off, a harbor. "One more, guys!" I shout. And then my eyes widen as I see the massive wave of our own wake bearing down on us. And I realize it's Tori's giant wave she kept talking about. "It's after this wave!"

Trey crawls to the table and wraps his arms around the post.

It feels like we're on a roller coaster. The wave picks the ferry up and rolls us way to one side and then pushes us, like a surfer, toward the shore, throwing more people off balance and onto the floor or crashing into tables.

We spin and ride the wave, and when we reach the bottom of it we feel the second jolt, and hear the groaning, grinding, shredding sound from the starboard side as the ferry lurches and shudders.

There is mass confusion, an emergency alarm goes off, and then a voice on the loudspeaker says something nobody can understand.

"Everybody okay?" I ask, trying to talk over the noise.

They nod. And I'm not going to lie—they all look scared shitless. Which is exactly how I feel.

"Okay. Let's go!" I shout. "Now!"

We stay low to keep better balance as we step over and around people and luggage as the ferry continues to ride crazily over waves. As we move toward the door to the outer deck, we tell everyone who will listen to grab the flotation devices under their seats.

Once outside we can hear the emergency message directing people to put on their life vests and head to the lifeboat muster stations, but I know the people inside can't understand a word of the message with all that noise. We form a human chain, with Ben and Trey hauling the life vests out of the bench seats and shoving them down at me and Sawyer. Rowan, who stands near the glassed-in area, passes them by the handfuls to people who need them as they begin to stream outside. We try to talk in calm tones whenever the voice on the loudspeaker stops, trying to help keep order, but it's nearly impossible. And the ferry keeps lurching and rolling on the waves. But we manage to find at least a few of our victims from the list and get life vests on them.

Finally we grab armloads of the remaining life preservers from the front deck and go back inside to try to find our victims and make sure they have them. We figure that most of the drowning victims are the people who were injured at the first impact, thinking they may be unable to get to a lifeboat. But none of our victims are where they were just minutes ago. Crew members are in sight, some sporting obvious injuries but helping people to the lifeboats anyway.

We split up. Rowan peels away from the group and heads to the first-class cabin, and from my list I spot the older couple with matching sweatshirts and rush over to them. The woman is lying on the deck and the man is on his hands and knees beside her, trying to stay in one place.

"Put this on," I say near the man's ear, indicating the life vest. "And then we'll get you two out of here, okay?"

He's in shock or something, and the woman just stares up at me. Her wrist is twisted at a strange angle, and she says her hip hurts and she can't sit up or walk.

I put the life vest over her head and slide the belt around her back the best I can without hurting her, and I put her husband's on him as well when it's clear he's unable to do it himself. And then I look for help.

"Ben!" I yell when I spot him. He turns and sees me. Soon he's kneeling next to us. "She can't walk. And he's . . . not really responding to anything. What do we do?"

He looks around, his rain-soaked hair whipping and sticking to his face. "Ah. There's one," he says. He gets up and grabs a backboard from the wall and lays it on the deck next to the woman. "Help me lift her," he says. "On three."

We get the woman on the board and Ben straps her

down. I spy my duffel bag and crawl over to it just as all lights except a few emergency ones go out. A cry goes up. Luckily, it's not dark out yet, but the clouds are keeping any sunlight from shining in. I can still see, but not well. I grab the rope and sling it around my arm, and crawl back to Ben.

"You're going to get this man on the lifeboat," Ben says, "and then we'll come back for her once it's cleared out a bit and we can maneuver the board, okay? I see two of my people—I'll be back." He grabs his stack of life vests and goes.

I take the man by the arm and lead him to one of the lifeboat stations as the emergency alarm drills into my head over and over again.

When I turn around, I'm climbing uphill, and I realize that the ferry must be already starting to list to one side. Every few minutes I feel the ferry shudder, and I think the cars below us must be shifting as water pours in. I fight panic and strain my eyes trying to find the rest of my people. I don't see any of them, but I catch a glimpse of Trey getting some of his people out.

"Jules!" Rowan screams from behind me, in the doorway to the first-class cabin. I turn and run over to her. "I got four of them out of here, but this guy . . ."

I look beyond her and see a man facedown on the conference table in a pool of blood and glass everywhere. "Oh my God," I say. "Is he dead?"

"I think so. There's glass stuck all in his head."

"Let's go—we'll tell Ben. Lifeguards can probably tell if someone's dead or not, right? I still need to find three of my people."

"Which ones?"

"Brown-haired small man with blue-and-white pinstripe shirt. Twentysomething woman with big earrings and hair in a bun. Light-blond, rosy-cheeked middle-aged man in a red Windbreaker."

"I saw Sawyer helping the woman with the earrings get into a lifeboat," Rowan says, peering around. "Let's check outside on the decks. They aren't in here."

The ferry shudders and tilts even more. We both instinctively drop to our hands and knees, slipping a little. A guy running past us totally biffs and falls over me. He gets up and keeps going, slipping and falling every few steps. Rowan looks at me. "We don't have much time."

We crawl at top speed to the outer deck. And there I see my little brown-haired man, without a life vest, jumping off the railing.

Forty-Five

"No!" I shout. I slide over to the railing and look out after him. "Shit!" I look at Rowan, knowing I need to go after this guy, but remembering the matching sweatshirt woman. "Ro! There's an older woman on a backboard not far from where we were sitting—Ben knows about her and will help you get her to the lifeboat. Don't worry about my red sweater guy. Just get the woman and then you get in that boat too, you hear me?" The ship groans and tilts more, and I slip on the wet deck and land on my back. "Shit." My panic shows in my voice. "Okay, Rowan?"

She can tell I'm freaked. "Okay, I promise! Are you going after him?"

"Yes, I have to. I'll be fine!" I whip my sweatshirt off

and toss my shoes aside, clip a life vest to one end of my rope, and then, without allowing myself to think, I climb the railing and balance there for a second, looking at the horrible scene below. Waves churning. The runaway empty lifeboat floating far away—we didn't even have a chance to try to save it. People struggling in the water and hanging on to the sides of the lifeboats, unable to climb in. It's a long enough drop to the water to give me pause.

I spot my little man in the water as the ferry shudders and tilts again. My foot slips off the railing, I lose my balance, and suddenly I'm falling. Before I can take a deep breath, I hit the water and keep going. The cold on my face makes me want to gasp, but I fight it, and before long my life vest has me popping up above the water again.

Wiping the water from my eyes, I get my bearings, and as a huge swell lifts me high, I see the little man. His head is tilted back and he's not yelling or trying to swim or struggling or anything, which Ben says is a major warning sign of drowning. I swim toward him as fast as I can, dragging my rope and extra life jacket with me. As I get closer, he bobs under the water and comes back up again.

"Sir!" I scream, unclipping the extra vest from my rope. "Take this!" I throw the life jacket at him and then swim the rest of the way as his head slips under the water again. I grab his shirt and lift him, and he grasps and clings to me and coughs, almost pulling me under the water. I thread the vest underneath his armpits to keep his face above the water, and I can only hope he can hang on, because I can't risk trying to get the thing on him the proper way.

My thighs burn and I'm out of breath. "Sir!" I yell in his face. "Hang on to this!" He manages a nod.

I strike out for the nearest lifeboat with the other end of the rope, checking over my shoulder every few seconds to make sure he's still there.

From here, the ferry looks huge and scary and completely misshapen as it sinks lower in the water, tilted at a strange, extreme angle. I can see the entire front deck, people crawling around trying to hang on. There's still one lifeboat attached to the ferry and being loaded, and as I push through the water I spot Rowan, Ben, and a crew member lowering the older woman on the board into the lifeboat using their ropes.

And then I see Sawyer on the rear deck railing, the blond girl with the polka-dot headband riding on his back. She must be injured. They're getting ready to jump. A wave of relief washes over me—she must be his last victim if he's going over the side with her. *Come on, Sawyer,* I think. *You can do this.* I send him all the mental energy I can muster to help him get past his fear and jump to safety.

I check on my guy, who is still hanging on. "We're almost there," I call out to him, and wind up with another mouthful of water as the tumultuous waves surround me. I am quickly growing exhausted. It's about all I can do right now to get to the lifeboat so the people in it can drag this man in. Finally I make it, and a woman grabs the rope from me and starts pulling. Others try to help me get in despite my protests, but the ferry groans and leans farther toward us, making everyone stop for a moment to stare.

And it keeps going, rolling slowly onto its side. "God in heaven," I whisper. I gasp and choke on water as the contents of the car ferry appear to shift drastically, the front end sinking faster than the back. The ferry tilts quickly now, to sixty degrees or so. The crew loosens their hold on the swinging lifeboat, and it drops sickeningly fast to the water. A second later, almost everyone else remaining on the deck falls too. I look around frantically for Trey and Rowan and Ben and Sawyer as the falling bodies surface. The water is dotted with a dozen passengers.

A woman in the lifeboat tugs at me. "No, I'm fine," I croak, not looking at her. "I'm going to help some of these people."

I search for the ones without life vests on, but it looks like everybody on my team did a fantastic job of doling them out, which gives me a surge of hope. I spy Trey in the water helping someone get to a lifeboat, and then I see that it's Rowan. My heart stops for a minute, but she is able to climb in on her own, so I think she's okay. She must have actually listened to me. Trey signals to somebody. I follow his gaze, and I see Ben swimming far out to save someone. As I ride up the next wave, I look for Sawyer, but I don't see him anywhere. "Sawyer!" I yell, but it's useless, because everybody else is yelling for people too.

I grab the rope and strike out toward a floating passenger, knowing we're still in a lot of danger. These people in the water don't have wet suits on. Just because they're not drowning at the moment doesn't mean they're safe. I sure as hell hope we're not relying solely on Ben's 911 call—there had to be others. Maybe somebody's fancy underwater car alerted OnStar. And of course there's the crew, who must have radioed for the Coast Guard. But I don't see anybody coming to our rescue. Lightning streaks across the sky and I realize it'll be totally dark soon.

I string two passengers together with the rope, and the woman in the lifeboat starts towing them in like a champ. Once I know they're good, I whip my head around, looking for anybody else who needs help, and I see the girl with the polka-dot headband. She no longer has the glasses she was wearing on the ferry. I swim toward her and she's just floating and crying, teeth chattering, in the water. "Come on," I say to her. "I'll help you."

I reach my arm out and she grabs on.

"What's your name?" I say. "I'm Jules."

"Bridget," she says. And then she mutters through her

tears, "As in, I wish there was a road from here to land so we could bridge it."

I can't help but smile. My mom would say this girl's got spunk.

I flip to my back and start kicking, pulling her with me, trying to get somewhere. But I'm losing steam. The rain pelts my face; it's warmer than the water I'm in. "We're headed for a lifeboat that has room for you. You doing all right?"

"I can't find my family," she says. "And I can't see very well. I lost my glasses."

I remember seeing her on board, and noting that the rest of her family was not on the victim list. "I'm sure they're fine. I'm positive, okay? I mean it. Hundred percent."

She nods, taking me at my word. "Okay."

"Are you hurt?"

"My ankle. It hurts really bad. I can't kick. That guy said it might be broken."

That guy. "That guy who was with you when you jumped?"

"Yeah."

"Where did he go?"

"I don't know," she says, her teeth chattering uncontrollably now. "He told me my job was to fight through the pain and swim to the lifeboat. And then he dropped me over the edge."

Sawyer, where the hell are you? My limbs are shaky and tired, and now that we're almost done here, I'm feeling the edge of the cold. My feet and face are getting numb.

I pull the girl toward the nearest lifeboat, where Rowan is, but the boat just seems to be floating farther and farther away in the waves. "Ro!" I shout. "Rowan!"

She turns and spots me. "Thank God!" she says. "We couldn't find you!"

"I'm fine, but do you have your rope you can throw us? She's freezing."

Rowan shakes her head, agitated. "It's with the lady on the board in a different boat." She looks around and apparently sees Trey on the other side of her boat. She calls to him, and a second later I see his rope flying through the air to her. She catches it, holds one end, and tosses the other one my way. I swim out to reach it and do my best to tie it to Bridget's life vest, but my fingers aren't cooperating.

It's when I'm stringing the rope through a fluorescent green loop on the vest that I realize it. My heart stops.

Bridget is wearing a life vest that looks exactly like mine.

"Where did you get this life vest?" I scream, my voice hoarse.

Bridget looks at me, scared. "The ferry was rolling onto its side and the guy made me take it. He said he could go back for another one."

I stare at her, my face in her face, and I have no words, only fear squeezing my lungs, suffocating me from inside my ribs.

Someone starts pulling Bridget to the lifeboat, and I flounder in the water as all light disappears, paralyzed in the murk.

I scream his name.

Scream it again, louder than the voice of the storm.

People in the boats stop to look at me.

Rowan stands up, and I catch the look of terror on her face, eyes wide in a flash of lightning. She joins me in yelling. "Sawyer!"

The woman from the first lifeboat yells for me too.

And then a man's voice.

Trey's voice.

But Trey is screaming a different name.

Forty-Six

Our screams are drowned out by thunder and groaning and engines and blades.

There are three full lifeboats and the one that got away. I don't know how many of the twenty-seven victims we saved, and I don't care. I am numb on the inside and hysterical on the outside.

"Invincible!" I scream. "You said!" I cry. "You said you wouldn't take it off!" But my voice is gone now.

What feels like hours later, I am lifted by strong arms and wrapped in a towel and put on a surface that doesn't move. We sit in a shadow. My sister holds my head and kisses it. Her tears drip on my tears.

My brother isn't screaming anymore on the outside. He leads us off the dock, away from the people. Even in our pain, we know we must be invisible. We escape cameras and paramedics and slip away to watch a helicopter shine a light on the water where a ferry used to be, searching for any signs of life. There are still people missing, the voices say over and over.

After a while, the light goes out.

We stare into the darkness, but there is no life out there.

Hours later, there is nothing we can do here. A bus takes my brother and sister and me to Milwaukee, and we get inside the not-delivery car with shaky hands and bare feet. When our doors are closed, Trey inserts the key, lets his forehead drop to the steering wheel, and sobs. And I cannot console him, because I am sobbing too.

And then we breathe, because we have to. And we hope, because there's nothing else to do.

We make a stop at Kate's because we don't have her phone number, tell her everything about the ferry disaster but not about the visions, and we let her decide what—and when—to tell Sawyer's estranged parents. We exchange phone numbers in case one of us hears something. And there's nothing we can do about Ben, whose mom and dad are in the Philippines visiting family.

It's well after midnight when we get home, and the lights are out. Rowan has taken care of Mom and Dad, bullshitting them about some major project we're apparently helping Trey with so he can win a scholarship. And they, tired from work and happy to hear we're so focused, have gone to sleep. We strip off our wet suits and dress in warm, dry clothes, and fall into bed, exhausted, phones in hands.

When I wake up with a start a little after five thirty, and then remember, the numbness inside of me is replaced by the most intense guilt, and I realize the extent of what I've done. Because I am responsible for this, too. I am responsible for all the world.

I crawl out of bed and knock softly on Trey's door, and then go in.

He's lying on his side in the dark, his face lit up by his phone, refreshing the news.

I stand in front of him. He doesn't look at me.

"I'm so sorry," I say.

His eyes twitch. His bottom lip quivers and then is still. Without a word, he opens up his arms, and I sit on the edge of his bed, and he holds me.

After a minute, he sits up and rubs his bleary eyes. And then he sighs. "It's not your fault."

I remain silent.

"If they're together, they're alive," he says after a while. "Ben is a lifeguard. Lifeguards don't drown. Even if that's not true, I have to believe it."

I swallow hard. I don't know how anybody could have

survived out there. "Ben has his phone, right?" I say. "Sawyer doesn't." *He broke his promise, and now he doesn't have his phone.*

"I think so." Trey looks at me. "What about Tori?"

I shrug. "I have a million texts from her. I haven't even started to read them."

"But wouldn't she know?"

"Know what?"

"Doesn't the vision change as the thing happens? Didn't you see body bags disappearing?"

I blink. And then I'm calling her, unable to breathe.

"Jules!" she says. "I'm so glad you're okay."

"Tori, listen to me. How did the vision change at the end? How many dead?"

"I texted you everything," she says. "Only three bodies."

"Who were they?" My throat constricts. I feel like I'm going to die if I don't get an answer immediately.

"I don't know—everything was dark in the vision at the end. I could only see dark shapes under the water."

"Can you pull it up and look at it? Get a closer look?" I ask, but I know the answer already.

"It's over, Jules," Tori says softly. "I can't. It's done."

Trey grips my hand.

"Sawyer and Ben are . . . missing," I say. "And I'm just wondering . . . do you think any of the bodies . . ."

She is silent. In shock. "I don't know. Oh my God, I'm so sorry. What can I do?"

I close my eyes. "Nothing. Just . . . send good thoughts. Or pray, or whatever you do."

She says something else comforting, but I don't comprehend it. "I can't talk right now," I say. I hang up. I never want to talk to her again. And then I look up at Trey.

"I don't know what to do," I say. "I'm just so sorry." The word drags itself from my gravelly throat and comes out like an oath. "I'm so *angry* . . . at myself. What was I thinking? How could I drag everybody into this? What the hell is wrong with me, Trey?"

He stares at a spot on the carpet for a long moment. And then he says, "You didn't drag anybody into this. We came willingly, knowing what could happen. You aren't in control of this thing." He looks up. "So if you're going to be mad at anybody, be mad at Dad. If he started it, then this is all his fault."

Forty-Seven

We want to stay home from school and stare at our phones, waiting for word, but we're already potentially in enough trouble. And really, if Sawyer or Ben calls, I have no problem barreling out of whatever class I'm in to answer him. So we go to school. By the time first hour is over, Sawyer and Ben have been missing for twelve hours.

I hear a few people talking about the ferry wreck, but there's no mention of Sawyer. People don't know he's missing . . . or possibly dead. And I don't want them to know. Because today, this grief belongs to me. And I don't want anybody infiltrating it with their fake-ass, disgusting bullshit.

After psych, Mr. Polselli asks me if I'm feeling all right. I don't want to cry, so I just nod and take off. At lunch Rowan sits with Trey and me at our usual table. We all look haggard and feel worse. My body is sore and I have bruises in weird places.

We can't seem to stay off our phones, checking the news, checking Chicago social media reports, seeing if Kate has heard from Sawyer, and both Trey and I get yelled at more than once in sculpting class. We accomplish nothing.

Trey checks the news once more in class and whispers, "There's a press conference scheduled with some new information. Three bodies pulled from the water."

My stomach drops. Before I can reply, Ms. White, the art teacher, walks over to our table and holds out her hands. "Hand them over."

I look up at her and feel all the blood draining from my face. "Please, no. We'll put them away, I promise."

"I've already asked you to put them away and you didn't listen." She sticks her hands closer. "Now, please."

Trey leans in. "We're having a little family emergency," he says in a soft voice. "I'm really sorry. You know we never do this otherwise. We're just hoping for some . . . some news."

The teacher hesitates, most likely because we look so horrible today, and finally relents. "Inside your backpacks, then. Don't let me see them again. You can check for news after class."

Phew. "Thank you," I say. "I'm sorry." We put our phones in our respective backpacks and fake like we're working on our vase projects as time slows down to a stop. I strain my ears, listening for my phone's vibration, but I don't hear anything. And I start to lose hope.

After class, there's nothing new. The press conference happens during last hour and reveals stuff we already know or suspected: The ferry was diverted because of the weather. On the way into the intended harbor, the ferry hit a sandbar, the engines cut, the pilot was injured, and the ferry smashed into a breakwall, which tore open the vessel. It began taking on water, and within forty minutes, the wreck had sunk. All but two passengers made it off the ferry. A third reportedly drowned while attempting rescue. They aren't releasing the names of the victims yet because families haven't been notified.

We three meet up after school. "One of them on the ferry was that guy in first class," Rowan says when Trey and I reach her locker. She shudders. "Ben said he was probably dead, and there was no time, so we had to leave him."

"So that's one of the three. But none of us saw Sawyer jump. The girl, Bridget, said he went back for another life vest . . . so maybe he never made it out. And I saw Ben swimming far off the rear end of the ferry. That's the last time anybody saw him. Could he be the third?"

Neither responds.

I want to die.

I think I really am losing my mind.

And speaking of that, I've put it off long enough. And I know what it's time to do. "I'm going to talk to Dad," I tell Trey and Rowan as we trudge to the car after school. "I don't care anymore what they do to me."

Forty-Eight

It was Food Truck Tuesday from eleven to one today at a nearby factory, which means Mom and Dad are home for a couple of hours to restock before heading out for the dinner hour. They're sitting at the kitchen table when we get home, having coffee and looking over some early sketches—plans for the new restaurant. It's still weird to see my dad acting like this. Like a normal human.

Trey and Rowan decide to stick by me, so I guess this is kind of an intervention. I can't even think right now. Part of me knows this is a bad idea, but I'm exhausted and sick and furious that my Sawyer is gone and my dad has done all these things to me, and I'm feeling reckless.

We walk into the kitchen.

Mom and Dad look up. "Oh, hi," Mom says. "I

thought you were our tomatoes being delivered." She smiles. "How was school?"

I stare at my dad. He looks nice today. His hair is smoothed back and his face looks healthy. Happy. My determination wavers.

But then I remember Sawyer, and how he wouldn't be dead right now if it weren't for my dad.

"I want to talk to you," I say.

My dad's face slackens. He looks at Mom. "She's pregnant," he says. He looks back at me. "You're pregnant?"

I have never hated him more than at this moment. "No!" I say, and I feel like I have no control over anything that is happening in my head right now. "Don't ask me that ever again!" My mouth screws up all weird and I fight hard not to cry.

"Oh, honey." Mom reaches out and touches my arm. She gives my dad a disapproving look, and he just sits there, probably trying to figure out why I'm falling apart. "He was kidding. Right, Antonio?"

My dad nods. "I'm sorry. That's not funny."

I don't even know who he is anymore. Since when does my dad joke? Since our house and restaurant burned to the ground, apparently. I can feel Trey and Rowan behind me, giving me strength.

I suck in a breath, trying to calm down. And then I say, "Can we talk about you and your, um, your . . . health problems? I want to know more about your depression and the hoarding and all that."

My dad leans back in his chair as if the questions threaten his personal space.

"Like," I continue, "I remember when it started—the hoarding—and I want to know why. I want you to tell me why it started. And if it's weird or crazy sounding, don't worry, just please tell me."

Mom frowns and lowers her gaze, turning slightly to look at my dad.

And he's got this strained, horrible look on his face, like I'm betraying him just by asking.

I refuse to look away.

Finally he nods toward Trey and Rowan and says in a low voice, "You told them?"

I stare. "What?" I have no idea what he's talking about.

He raises his voice a little, sounding stern now. "Did you tell them?"

I'm confused. Does he already know he passed the vision curse to me? "You mean," I say, my voice faltering, "about the visions?"

He leans forward, an intense, questioning look on his face. "The *what*?" He looks at Mom and back at me. "The *what*?" he repeats.

My lips part, then close again. "Wait. What are *you* talking about?"

"You're the one who has something to talk about," he says. "I want to know if you told them. If they know what you told me. That day you quit the restaurant."

And it hits me like a ton of bricks. He thinks I told Trey and Rowan about his affair. I press my hand to my eyes. And my hand slides away and I look at him again, at the hurt in his eyes. "No, Dad," I say softly. "That's not my story to tell."

I can feel the awkwardness penetrating the back of my brain as Trey and Rowan shift on their feet. When the doorbell rings, Trey hastily pulls Rowan with him to answer it.

Mom stands up. "That's probably our farmer with the tomatoes," she says like she's relieved to be squeezing past me and following Trey and Rowan.

When they're gone, I shake my head. "I can't believe this is what we're talking about, Dad. Is that really it? Your affair? That's what set off the hoarding and the depression? The years of us never knowing if we were going to come home to find that you killed yourself?"

He looks at me, pain washing over his face, making him look old again. "Depression is a disease," he says. "But the affair, the recipe that Fortuno stole—those things ruined my life."

I feel fury rising up so fast I can't stop it. "No, Dad. You own those things. That stuff didn't have to ruin your life. You just let it."

He takes it. And then he nods. "Maybe."

I let out a breath. "Okay."

He hesitates, and lowers his eyes. His big fingers lace together on the table and he taps his thumbs a few times. "So," he says, "you're seeing visions? What's that about?"

I stare at him. But before I can say anything, I hear the floor creak behind me, and my dad's gaze flits to a spot over my shoulder. Dad's eyes narrow the slightest bit, and then he frowns and says in rough voice, "What happened to you?"

I whirl around.

Standing in the kitchen doorway is a boy.

A boy with deep green eyes the color of the sea, and thick black lashes.

A boy with matted-down hair, wearing strange clothes, and wrapped in a blanket.

My lip quivers. "You're not the tomatoes." And when I throw myself into his arms, he collapses to the floor, and we lie there, sobbing together.

Forty-Nine

As my dad shakes his head and steps over us, apparently unconcerned, or mistaking our crying for laughter, Sawyer reaches up and holds my face with his cool hands and looks into my eyes. "Ben's here too," he rasps. His voice is gone.

I roll off him and my eyes threaten to start crying all over again. "Are you okay?"

He nods. "I am now."

"I'll be right back," I say, feeling heartless, but having to see for myself. I take off for the living room, where Trey and Ben are locked in an embrace that looks like it may never end. I wrap my arms around them both and kiss Ben on the cheek, and then I kiss Trey on the cheek too. And I have no words for how this feels right now.

Rowan, the come-through champion, is somehow giving Mom an explanation of what's happening. I have no idea if she's making up some story or going with the truth here, and I don't even care. I run back to Sawyer, who is still on the floor in the kitchen doorway. He smiles up at me through half-closed lids. He looks rough.

"Let's get you home to bed," I say.

"But I'm so tired. . . . I wanna sleep in your bed with you." He slings an arm over his eyes. "Please?"

"Um, somehow I don't think that's going to be okay with the parentals. How about the couch?"

He nods and strains to get up.

"Does Kate know you're okay?"

"Yeah, Trey just texted her for me. I don't have my phone." He starts crawling toward the living room.

"I *know* you don't have your phone, you big jerk. What happened to you promising not to take your stupid life vest off? We had a deal!"

"I just knew you were going to yell at me," he says glumly.

We round the corner and see that the couch is already occupied by Ben.

"Oh no." Sawyer says. He looks longingly at the cushions, then collapses on the floor and lies there. It's like he's drunk with exhaustion or something.

"So what happened to you guys?" I say. "Have you slept at all?"

"In the taxi."

"You took a taxi here? Why the heck didn't you call?"

"I don't know anybody's phone numbers. Tried to get people on the street to let me google your landline, but they pretty much took one look at the two of us and ran. When I finally got the taxi driver to look the number up for me, he just wrote it down and wouldn't let me use his phone at first. I guess we look like scary, drug-addicted homeless guys." He takes a breath. "Later I finally convinced him I wasn't going to steal it and I called, but I got the recording."

"But—" I sputter. "But what about Ben? Didn't he have his phone?"

"No," he says sadly. "It fell in the water because I'm a loser."

"You're not a loser, you just need to fucking learn how to swim," Ben says in a muffled voice from the couch. "It's really not that hard."

But Sawyer doesn't respond. A moment later, I realize he's asleep.

I look at Rowan and Trey, and we don't know what to think. Finally I shrug and go into our bedroom, pull blankets from our beds to drape over them, and give Sawyer my pillow. All we can do is hang around and wait and make up more crazy shit to answer our parents' questions about why Ben and Sawyer are crashed out in the living room.

When it becomes clear that Ben and Sawyer are down for the night, we three Demarcos go to bed early, since we're exhausted too, and everyone sleeps until morning, when we finally get to hear the whole story.

Fifty

Rowan and I get up at five to take showers and make some breakfast. When I tiptoe past Sawyer, he grabs my foot and scares the crap out of me.

"Hey," he says. He eases his way to his feet with a little help from me, and gives me a long hug. He follows me to the kitchen and sits by the table. "I just need to be near you," he says in his hoarse voice.

By six forty-five, all five of us are sitting around the kitchen table.

"I'm so hungry," Sawyer says. "I have never been this hungry in my entire life." He shovels a forkful of scrambled eggs and a biscuit into his mouth, and Ben chows down as well. While they eat, I fill them in on what happened on our end, and how Tori couldn't tell who the three dead people were, and how the news practically confirmed to us that it must have been Sawyer and Ben who had drowned.

"But I didn't give up hoping," Trey says. "By the way, information about the three dead was released this morning. They were the guy with the glass in his head, some woman I can't figure out from the victim list, and the pilot, who I don't think was even on Tori's list, unless he looked like one of the other passengers. I don't know what happened there."

"We must have confused something," I say. "I'm sad three people died, but that means we saved twenty-four. And our boys are alive, which means more than anything."

Sawyer squeezes my thigh under the table.

"So tell us everything," I say. "I saw you with the girl with the polka-dot headband up at the railing, but then I looked away and you were gone."

"Ah, Bridget," Sawyer says. "What a piece of work that girl is. I'm sure her ankle was broken but she was a total trouper."

"Yeah, I noticed that. I also noticed the life vest she was wearing." I give him a patronizing smile.

"Okay, look," Sawyer says, wiping his mouth with a napkin and sitting back. "What do you want me to do? Throw a thirteen-year-old girl with a broken ankle out into the water without one? The ferry was rolling onto its side, and there was no time, and I'd already given out all the ones I was carrying. I figured once I had her safely in the water, you guys would take care of her, and I could more easily get another life vest without her on my back. So I gave her mine. And I'm not sorry, because according to the death list, she's not on it."

"But *you* almost were," I say. "I'm not letting this one go. I have to be able to trust you."

He sighs. "Fair enough. Anyway, I dropped her down into the water and then tried to scale the deck, but the ferry tilted even farther until I felt like I was trying to climb straight up. And just when I'd almost made it to one of the benches with the life vests inside, the ferry shifted hard and rolled, and I lost my grip and slid down the decline, hitting the railing and flipping over it into the water." He scrunches his eyes shut for a moment and gingerly rubs the nape of his neck. "That sucked bad. Good thing I have such a hard head."

"I saw him go over," Ben says. "I was in the water on that end of the ferry. I thought he might be knocked out, because he hit the railing pretty hard. So I swam out there and saw him flailing and realized he didn't have his life vest on. So I grabbed him and started looking for debris to hang on to."

"But," Sawyer says, "it was almost dark by then, so we had to rely on lightning to see anything."

Ben continues. "I decided our best option was to try to

make it to the breakwall we'd hit, even though the waves were washing over it at the mouth of the channel. I could see the higher part of it, and that was closer to us than the lifeboats at this point. But then we got caught in a riptide that took us out even farther away from you guys, and honestly, I thought that was going to be the end of us. I was tired, hanging on to Sawyer, and trying to coach him on what to do without losing all of my energy talking."

"Never fight against a riptide," Sawyer says wisely. "Swim perpendicular to it, parallel to the shore."

"Very good," Ben says. "Now learn how to swim."

"Anyway," Sawyer says. "So by the time we get out of the riptide we're really far from the ferry and from you guys, and Ben's trying to conserve energy because he's got to keep my face above water, and I'm trying not to freak out and make it worse. *Then*," he says with a sardonic smile, "we make a brilliant decision to get Ben's phone out and call for help. So he tries to keep his life vest above water and I try to get it out, except my hands are numb. I manage to get the phone out without it getting too wet, and as I'm trying to hold it above the water and get to the phone page, I fumble it, and it bounces off Ben's vest and plops into the water. And I am a loser."

"Dude, seriously. I kinda figured that would happen. But we had to try. We weren't going to make it."

Sawyer nods. "It was pretty frightening." He pauses

and looks up. "I really thought Ben was going to have to let me go any minute. We were both freezing and exhausted and running out of hope."

Trey, Rowan, and I are spellbound. I'm gripping my fork so tightly my knuckles are white. "What happened?"

Sawyer leans forward. "But then there's more lightning. And poof."

"Poof," Ben says, nodding.

"Poof?" Trey asks. "What the hell does that mean?"

Fifty-One

"It means poof! The sky lights up, and there, not forty yards away, is that runaway lifeboat," Ben says.

"No way," Rowan says under her breath.

"Yeah way," Ben says.

"Hey, let's not bring God into this," Trey says.

I laugh because I'm a dork, but Ben ignores the joke and continues. "So then I have to decide if we should try to rest for a few minutes first by floating on our backs, and then strike out, or if we just go for it so it doesn't get farther away. And ultimately, I don't want to risk losing it, so I get Sawyer to kick his lazy-ass feet and hang on to my vest belt, and I flip over and start swimming breaststroke like my life depends on it, which it does, out in ten-foot waves trying to catch a lifeboat."

"It took us forever," Sawyer says. "I watched the heli-copter leave—it never swept the light out as far away as we were. By the time Ben got us to the lifeboat, he was practi-cally dead. I climbed in and hauled him up. He saved my life." He turns and looks at Ben. "You saved my life, man, and I will never forget it."

"Now we're even," Ben says lightly.

There's a quiet moment while *that* sinks in.

"But how did you guys survive the night?" I ask. "It was cold, and you were wet—how are you not frozen or hypothermic or dead?"

Ben and Sawyer exchange a glance and a small smile. "Body heat," Sawyer says with a shrug. "Skin-on-skin contact."

Trey stands up, his chair hitting the wall. "What?" he screeches. "That is . . . holy crap," he says, softer. "That's a picture, is what that is. Mmm."

"It was super-romantic," Sawyer says.

I bite my lip.

"Naaah, we're just kidding," Ben says after a beat. "The lifeboat had supplies in it. Blankets and hand warm-ers. Stuff like that." He grins as Trey sits back down. "But I did get to see his junk."

"Easy there, sailor," Sawyer says. "Don't spoil the sur-prise for the ladies."

Rowan laughs and then pouts. "I never get to see junk. Not fair."

"Fake boyfriend," I cough into my hand.

"Shut it," Rowan says. She turns to Ben. "So was there a flare gun or whatever? How did you get to shore?"

"Well, the helicopter was long gone by the time we got into the lifeboat. So we rested for a while first, and then we went into supersleuth mode and decided that we were out of immediate danger, and that life in general would go much smoother for Sawyer if his parents didn't ever find out he was on a ferry wreck on a school day. And my parents are out of the country, so I wasn't too worried about any news getting back to them very quickly."

Sawyer looks at me. "And I figured the last thing you'd do would be to go to my parents to tell them I'm missing, and that you'd go to Kate first to see what she thought, and she'd most likely want to wait to say anything until we knew for sure what was happening, because of the way my father tends to overreact."

"You know us pretty well," I say. "Though I'll bet Kate was on the verge of telling them when you guys landed on the doorstep."

Sawyer nods. "Yeah, I wouldn't blame her. Anyway, we decided the best plan would be to paddle to a pier or a jetty, put our wet suits back on, ditch the lifeboat, and walk to the beach like we were out just having fun."

"By then the rain had stopped," Ben says, "and the wind started calming down. It was just a matter of time before the lake would be easier to manage. So once we rested and got warm and ate some weird freeze-dried food and crackers we found in the lifeboat, the sun was coming up, so we could see where we were heading. We started paddling toward that bird sanctuary out there on the harbor north of Chicago. When we got close, we put our wet suits on again and I made Sawyer wear the life vest all the way into the park in case he fell headfirst into a bucket of water or something."

"Well played," Sawyer says, and they do some secret fist-bump handshake thing I've never seen them do before.

"We hailed a cab not far from the beach," Ben says. "Sawyer used the driver's phone to call your landline, but just got the recording that Demarco's Pizzeria is rebuilding and will reopen this fall."

"We didn't hook up the residential number when we moved here since we all had cell phones," Trey murmurs. "And those numbers aren't listed."

Ben nods. "I'm just glad I still had my wallet. It was a bit wet after the phone ordeal, but obviously the credit card still worked, and that's all that matters." He checks the clock on the wall and frowns. "The driver dropped us at my dorm and waited so we could quickly change into some clothes, and then took us straight here." He looks at Trey and reaches for his hand. "We couldn't wait to get here. It was so frustrating how lost we were, not having anybody's contact information memorized. I always had it there in my phone. And now it's at the bottom of Lake Michigan."

I notice Ben checking the time, and reluctantly I stand up, because we need to go. "Sawyer, do you want to go to school or just go home?"

"I want to go where you go."

Ben says, "My only class today starts in ten minutes, so I think I'm skipping one more day." He grins. "You want me to hang out here and wait for you?" he asks Trey. What a guy.

"Um, no." Trey looks sidelong at Rowan. "You wanna be Mom and call in sick for me?"

Rowan smirks. "How much is it worth to you?"

Fifty-Two

Trey drops Rowan, Sawyer, and me at Kate's. Sawyer brushes his teeth and grabs his backpack, and we take his car to school. Trey takes a sick day and spends it with Ben. Mr. Polselli checks in with me and I give him a bright smile. Lunch is intimate, just Sawyer and me, and we hold hands across the table as he tells me all the places on his body that hurt so I can feel sorry for him. In sculpting, Ms. White asks me if Trey and I got the news we were hoping for.

"We did," I say, and I can't stop smiling. I decide to work extra hard on my vase today to thank Ms. White for being lenient. And maybe I'll even pull off a better grade on it than Trey, which would rock.

After school, Sawyer drops Rowan and me off at our

house so he can go home, rest for a bit, and catch up on his homework.

And there's my dad, sitting in the living room with the shades drawn and the TV on at three o'clock in the afternoon.

Rowan gives me a look of doom. My stomach drops. The stretch of good times is over. Did I do this to him?

He looks up when we walk through the room on the way to our bedroom. "Girls!" he booms. "How was your day?"

I freeze. And slowly turn to look at him. "Fine," I say.

"Good. Rowan, your mother wants you to help her in the backyard. She's planting a garden so we can grow our own stuff for the food truck."

Rowan's eyes widen. "Oh. Okay." She drops her backpack in the bedroom and escapes out of here like a sidewinder.

Dad turns the TV off and reaches back to open the blinds behind the couch. "I was just killing time waiting for you to get here." He's shaved and showered and nicely dressed as usual for the past few weeks. "We never finished talking yesterday."

"Oo-kay," I say. I slide my backpack off my shoulder and lower my body to perch on the edge of the couch next to him.

"Your mother told me I need to communicate more,

and that I should tell you that we, ah, we like your friends. And that it's nice to have them come over, and at first we weren't used to having them in the house, but now it . . . it's nice. Because then we know where you are, and . . . well. She told me to tell you that."

I raise an eyebrow. "So you like Sawyer now?"

He shifts uneasily. "I . . . yes, I think he's okay. Your mom said he's not living at home."

I tilt my head. "Oh, I get it. He's having problems with his parents, so you like him more because of that."

"That's not what I meant. That's not fair. I tell you something nice and you throw it in my face." He fidgets with his hands and I can tell he's getting defensive.

I choose to let it go since he seems to be trying to be a better . . . whatever. "Okay. I'm sorry. I'm glad you like our friends."

"Also," he goes on, his face pained, "you told me I needed to own my mistakes, and I've been thinking about that. And even though your mother has been telling me that for years, hearing it from you seemed, well, different. It made me feel . . . ashamed."

I don't know where this is going, and I don't know what to say.

"I decided I'm going to go see somebody. A therapist," he says. "Your mom's coming with me."

"Oh," I say. "Oh. Well, that's great. I mean, I hope . . ." I trail off. What is the appropriate response to this statement? I don't know.

"Yeah," Dad says, his gaze drifting to the window, where we can barely see Mom laughing with Rowan and digging up the lawn. "I hope it's good, but I don't know. We'll see."

"Sure. Of course." I want to fall through this couch and through the floor and through the earth's crust and disappear. "Well, thanks for telling me." My body aches to stand and walk away, but my butt is glued to this cushion.

"And so, thank you. And for not saying anything to Trey and Rowan. I appreciate that. I—I think I'm going to tell them soon, but I want to ask the therapist first."

Who ARE you? I swear I am in an alternate reality right now. There's no way this can last.

"That brings me to my next question," he says. "Why did you ask me about the health stuff?"

My head grows light. "No reason," I say. I shift my weight farther onto the cushion, not because I want to relax and chat, but because I'm teetering on the edge of it and could fall at any time.

"Why did you ask me about visions?"

I glance at his face and see him looking earnestly into mine. And I still can't read his expression. Is he asking me because he wants to confess that he has seen visions too?

Or because he's worried that I have, and he wants to put me in an asylum?

"I don't know," I say, scrambling. "I guess I've seen you staring off into space, and you don't drive much, and we've got the whole mental illness thing in the family with Grandpa Demarco, so I thought I'd . . . ask."

He regards me thoughtfully. "Are you asking because of . . . anything personal that's happening with you? Do you need to talk to a doctor?"

Ugh. I wish he'd just answer. "Well, I'm not pregnant, if that's what you're asking."

He chuckles. "I said I was sorry about that. It really was a joke this time."

I feel the residual resentment boiling up again. "Yeah, well, you're very different lately and hard to read, and you're telling jokes now, so I guess I just don't know how to talk to you." I can feel my face getting hot.

He looks down. "I know. I'm sorry." He scratches his head and says softly, "Losing the house and the restaurant . . . losing all of that stuff . . ." He shakes his head. "I was suffocating at first. But then suddenly starting from nothing became this opportunity . . . I don't know. Like the chains came off my wrists." He rests his head in his hands for a moment. "I hated the hoarding, but I couldn't stop it. I was compelled to continue. I couldn't break the cycle." He reaches into his pocket and pulls out the thimble from the Monopoly game. He shows it to me. "This is what I chose to keep from the remains of the fire. The only thing."

I don't tell him that Trey and I watched him take it.

"When I was a kid, I used to play Monopoly with Mary and my dad. Whenever we landed on the income or luxury tax spaces, or had to pay to get out of jail, instead of paying the bank, we put the money in the middle of the board under the thimble. And if you landed on Free Parking, you won it—you got to take the money. It was the absolute best when it happened on your last turn before you ran out of money, facing all those houses and hotels in the Marvin's Gardens row. Hitting it just right—it gave you new life. A chance to change the game, my dad said." He looks at me. "All of that junk and the emotional baggage was dragging me down. And losing everything in the fire . . . well, that turned out to be my Free Parking. My chance to change the game. So even though it'll probably be really hard, I'm going to take it. I am taking it."

I nod, absorbing it all. It's amazing how much happens to the people around me when I'm not paying attention.

He reaches over and squeezes my hand. "I was a pretty good dad back before the dark days. I want to get better at being your dad again."

I had no idea my dad could speak so eloquently, and

I'm actually moved by this. Jules is reluctantly impressed. I place my other hand on top of his. "I just want you to feel good," I say. "Every day."

He leans over and kisses my cheek. "Me too."

And as we sit there, contemplating changes, the biggest question in my life remains. I still don't know for sure if he has seen a vision—he never answered the question. I still don't have any of the answers I need.

I am happy that he wants to be a better dad. But I am also tired, and I am sick of seeing people I love get hurt. I just want this trail of visions to end. I just want him to say no, he's never seen a vision, so that I can remove this responsibility from my shoulders and call it quits on this game of madness. Because if I don't find out for sure, I'm going to have to start trying to find the twenty-four people we saved and begin this stupid process all over. And I know I can't do this again.

So after all of that, I just say it. "Okay, well, back to the question, just to clear things up. Have you ever had a vision or not?"

Fear and concern flit across his face. And then he says, "I'm not sure why you're so fixated on this. But the answer is no, Julia. I have issues that I'm working on, but I'm not that far gone. I've never seen a vision." He hesitates and then frowns. "Have you?"

I look into his eyes, and I know he's telling the truth.

And I feel a surge of hope. Part of me feels a tremendous weight being lifted at the sudden realization: there is no Demarco vision curse.

But then I realize this only makes me look more insane. Does this mean that *I* am the true source of this vision curse? And does this make me even more responsible than before, now that I have no one to point to?

Before I can say a word to deflect his new concerns, my cell phone vibrates.

It's Sawyer—Sawyer's phone, rather—calling me.

Fifty-Three

"Of course not, don't be silly," I tell my dad, then point to the phone. "Mind if I take this?"

"Go for it. I'll be outside helping your mother," he says, which is so weird. He pats my hand and gets up.

I answer on the fifth ring. "Hello?" I say.

"Hi," comes a girl's self-assured voice. "Is this the Jules from the lake?"

I almost laugh. "Yes! Is this the Bridget with the sore ankle?"

"It's broken," she says, as if she's pleased about it. "I'm on crutches."

"Oh no," I say. "I was afraid of that. How did you figure out to call me?"

"Well," she says, "by the time I found my parents and

brother, I didn't see the guy anywhere to give the phone back to him. And by the time we got to our hotel from the emergency room, the battery was dead, and we don't own a charger to fit this kind of phone. So I had my brother buy one with the twenty bucks I also found in the pocket. And now, duh, it's working again."

"Wow," I say. "You definitely have spunk." This is quickly becoming an easy word to use.

"And," she rambles on, "I remembered how you pretty much screamed at me when you saw me wearing this life vest, and yours was just like it, so I figured you must know the guy. And I remembered you said your name was Jules. So I looked in the contacts and found you at the top. Are you his girlfriend or something?"

"Um, well, yes." I'm blushing.

"Well, can you tell him I've got his phone?"

I laugh. "Yes, I will tell him. How can we get it back from you?"

"One sec." She yells away from the mouthpiece, "Hey, Ma!"

I can hear muffled sounds of the mouthpiece against fabric, and then she's yelling something to her mom.

She comes back. "Where does the guy live?"

It occurs to me that she hasn't yet figured out *the guy's* name. "His name is Sawyer. We live in Melrose Park outside of Chicago."

"One sec," she says again. More hollering.

I walk over to the window to watch Rowan and my parents dig up the lawn for a garden. "What the heck is happening to us?" I mutter.

Bridget comes back. "Okay, my parents said we can bring it over tonight. Text me your address when we hang up."

I'm confused, and then I realize she means for me to text it to Sawyer's phone. "Sounds great," I say.

"Okay, bye."

Before I can ask if her family is okay, she hangs up.

I text my address to Sawyer's phone for Bridget, and then text Kate to see if Sawyer is with her.

A minute later Sawyer calls me from Kate's phone. "What's up?"

"Bridget is coming to my house to bring your phone back. Can you come over?"

"How excellent. I was just missing you enough to come over anyway. Yeah, I'll be there in a few."

I smile. "Cool. Also. My dad just told me he thinks you're okay."

"Well." He sounds pleased. "That's something."

When Sawyer arrives, we sit on the front steps waiting for Bridget. Rowan comes around the house and sits with us. Her hands are dirty.

"Dad thinks you need to see a therapist," she announces. She looks at her dirty fingernails and scowls. "Yick. What a mess."

"Great," I say. "Well, at least I finally got a straight answer out of him. He says he's never seen a vision."

Sawyer turns, a consternated look on his face. "Is he telling the truth?"

"I think so."

"Whoa," Rowan says.

"I know." I stare at the ants digging a home in the crack in the sidewalk. "So I don't know what this means, except that I really did start it. I can't blame it on anybody else." I pause, and then I say decisively, "But the ferry was the last straw. We're done. I'm done. It's too dangerous, and I can't go through this anymore." I sigh, thinking about the prospects. "Besides, I can't track down twenty-four strangers to see who might be next. I'm just . . . I'm so *fuh-rucking* tired of it," I say. My eyes burn and I press the palms of my hands against them. "I can't do it anymore."

Sawyer pulls me close and kisses the side of my head. "You're right," he says softly. "It's too dangerous. Whatever this is, it's bigger than us. It's out of our control. And contrary to my statement several days ago, after going through that ferry ordeal I no longer believe we are invincible."

"So . . . we're done?" Rowan says.

I nod. "We're done. I'm calling it. It's over."

It's a relief to say it. Rowan texts Trey to let him know our decision, and he replies: *Aw, shucks. I want to see how many more ways we can DIE.* Then he follows up with: *Secretly, good call.*

We sit in silence, contemplating everything we've been through, when a car drives up. It occurs to me that it would be awkward if my parents witnessed this exchange, so I stand up and walk to the car. Sawyer and Rowan follow.

The parents get out, and then Bridget does too, slower, using her crutches. She's wearing new retro cat-eye glasses.

"I'm Alan Brinkerhoff," Bridget's dad says. "This is my wife, Emily, and I think you know Bridget." Bridget waves awkwardly, acting shy in the presence of her parents.

He reaches out to shake our hands.

"I'm Jules," I say, deciding there's no need for last names on our end—anonymous is a better way to go. "This is Sawyer, and this is Rowan."

"We want to thank you," Mrs. Brinkerhoff says, "for helping Bridge. I still don't know how we got separated. When I realized she wasn't with us, I nearly gave up. Everybody was shoving and pushing . . ." She shakes her head, remembering.

"No problem," Sawyer says. "She was really brave.

I'm sure her jump into the water hurt really bad with that ankle."

Bridget's ivory cheeks turn red. She reaches into the backseat of the car and holds out Sawyer's life vest. "Here ya go," she says, shoving it at him. She reaches back in again and hands him his cell phone and the charger.

Sawyer looks puzzled. "I didn't have my charger with me," he says.

"I know," Bridget replies, "but you bought one later with your twenty bucks."

"I see," Sawyer says.

I grin. "Thanks for driving it all the way over here. Do you guys live nearby?"

"No," Mr. Brinkerhoff says. "We live in Michigan, but we come to Chicago every now and then."

"I have cancer," Bridget says matter-of-factly. "I go to the University of Chicago for tests and treatment and stuff. I've had it my whole life."

"Well, not quite," Bridget's mother says.

"I was born with it."

"You were five," Mrs. Brinkerhoff says. "Stop making things up."

Bridget grins at me.

"Wow, I'm sorry," I say. My head is spinning. *Cancer?*

Mr. Brinkerhoff continues where he left off, like he's used to Bridget's interruptions. "Normally, we drive around the lake to get here, but we thought it would be fun to take the car ferry once."

"Fun!" Bridget snorts. "And now we don't have a car," she says. "It totally sank. Probably has fish in it by now. So we got this rental. It's pretty cool. It has a plug for my iPod in the backseat."

"Cool," Rowan says.

"Yeppers," Bridget says. She bobs her head and looks around. "Huh. Nice little place you got here."

I stifle another laugh. This girl is a hoot.

"Well," Sawyer says to Mr. Brinkerhoff, "thanks for driving out here to bring it to me. That was really nice of you."

"It's the least we could do. We'd really love to do something more for you," Mrs. Brinkerhoff says. "Maybe take you out for dinner or something . . ."

Inwardly I recoil. They're nice and everything, and Bridget is mildly hilarious, but I don't really want to have a relationship with these people. "Maybe," I say. "But we only did what anybody would do."

"I don't think so," Mrs. Brinkerhoff says. "Did you miss all the pushing and shoving, and the people stealing other people's life vests? It was a nightmare. You guys and your calm process—not to mention helping others before yourselves—you probably saved a lot of people."

"Yeah," Bridget says. "It was almost like you knew

it was going to happen." She tilts her head and flashes a charming smile, then shoves a stick of gum into her mouth.

I freeze. Sawyer gives a hollow laugh. But the moment of panic passes.

Mrs. Brinkerhoff reaches out and gives me a hug. "Bridget wrote down your number—I hope that's okay."

I plaster a smile on my face. "Oh, how clever of her. Sure. Call anytime."

After another round of thanks, they get back into the car and Mr. Brinkerhoff presses buttons on the dashboard, probably entering their next destination into the GPS. We walk back to the step and watch them pull away. And then they stop.

The back door to the car opens and Bridget gets out, without her crutches this time. "Yo, Jules!" she yells. She hops on one foot across the yard toward us. I stand up and go toward her.

"What's up? Did you forget something?" I ask.

"Yeah, I forgot to give you a hug."

Kids these days. I try not to roll my eyes, and I lean down so she can hug me.

She wraps her arms around my neck and puts her mouth to my ear. And then she whispers, so softly I can barely hear her, "Guess what? I know about the vision."

Before I can say a word, she's hopping back to the car

and closing the door, and I'm watching them drive off, wondering, for the millionth time, if I'm losing my mind.

"She knows about the vision," I tell Sawyer and Rowan once their car is out of sight.

"What?" Rowan asks. "How?"

I think about it for a long moment. "She must have read our text messages on your phone, Sawyer. I wouldn't put it past her."

"I don't think anyone would believe her if she, you know, went to the media or something," Sawyer says. "Did she say it threateningly? Or what?"

"No," I say. "Just matter-of-factly, like she blurts out everything else."

"It probably just makes her feel cool," Rowan says. "I read your texts all the time. Makes me feel supercool."

I punch her in the shoulder. "You'd better not."

"Psh. Good luck trying to stop me."

Sawyer rolls his eyes. "Anyway. If she wasn't threatening, then I doubt we have to worry about it."

"Me too." I look sidelong at Rowan. "Do you really read my texts? That's gross."

She frowns. "Of course not. Don't be a douche."

Later, after Sawyer goes home and everybody is safe in their beds and Bridget Brinkerhoff is but a memory, my phone vibrates with a text message. I think it might be

Tori, so I scramble to check it because I forgot to tell her Sawyer and Ben are fine.

But it's not Tori.

It's a message from a strange number I don't have programmed into my phone. One I don't recognize. I open it and read: *Hey Julesies! Guess what? Now I'm seeing a vision too!*

Epilogue

Five weeks later.

It takes a four-eyed, hilariously blunt thirteen-year-old kid with cancer to point out the logic of the visions to me. And it's not until after we deal with her vision disaster that we realize we've hit a dead end.

As it turns out, Bridget Brinkerhoff is probably the best of all of us at solving the clues and carrying out the risky actions inside a vision. Maybe it's because she has to face death on a regular basis that she's so fearless. And maybe she's just faking bravery, like the rest of us. But Sawyer and I, Trey and Ben, Rowan, and probably even Rowan's not-fake Internet boyfriend, Charlie, would all agree that Bridget has a knack for figuring out what's in store for our little world. She's in remission now, by the way—a detail she nearly forgot to tell us after her last doctor's visit.

Bridget's vision? Stadium bleachers collapse at a graduation ceremony. At one point or another in the vision, she saw each of us dead, along with dozens of strangers.

But it's over now and here we are: Trey, Rowan, Sawyer, Ben, Bridget, and me. All still alive. We lie on our backs in the grass next to our garden, staring up at the stars.

"We could go try to get the graduating class list. Narrow down the possibilities to try to find the next person with the vision." It hurts my stomach to say it.

"It wouldn't help much, since none of the graduates were in those bleachers," Sawyer says. He holds my hand.

"Yeah, but maybe their families were."

"Extended families, friends," Trey says, "plus other students. Over a thousand of them. Face it, Jules. Unless the person finds us, we're done here. The vision curse moves on without us."

I close my eyes, wishing it to be true.

Bridget props herself up on an elbow. "So, I've been meaning to ask, who'd you get *your* vision from, Jules?"

"Nobody. I started it," I say.

Bridget snorts. "You did not."

I open my eyes and turn my head to look at her. "How would you know?"

"Ego much?" She grins.

I rip up a handful of grass and throw it at her face.

She laughs again and says, "No, come on. Really. Who'd you get your vision from?"

"I'm not joking," I say. "I really think it started with me. I haven't been in any tragedies."

"Well, when did your vision start?" she prods.

Rowan props up on her elbow too, on the other side of Bridget. "Yeah, when exactly did it start? Do you remember?"

Slowly everybody else shifts to look at me. "Suddenly I feel like I'm on a talk show," I say. I try to remember. "I don't know. I had my vision for a long time. Several weeks."

"If we work backward from the night before Valentine's, when the crash happened," Sawyer says, "where would that put you—first of the year, maybe?"

"Christmas," I say, thinking hard. "In fact, it was Christmas Day. We went to a movie—Trey, Rowan, and me. That first vision was in the theater."

"You're sure?" Ben asks.

I think harder. "Yes."

"So if it follows a pattern," he continues, "you would have been saved from some tragedy a day or two before, right?"

"I guess," I say. "But like I said, I wasn't—"

"Well, maybe somebody just did such a great job of saving you that you didn't even know you were saved," Bridget says.

Trey sits up. He starts to speak, and then he stops,

hand poised in the air as if he was about to make a point. And then he looks at me. "Wait," he says softly, closing his eyes, his face concentrating. "Wait a second." His eyes pop open. "When did you get mugged?"

Sawyer sits up in concern. "You got mugged?"

But I can't answer Sawyer because I'm thinking hard. "Christmas Eve, wasn't it, Trey? Or the night before that? But it was no big deal. Nothing really happened. The guy ran off when another guy came out of nowhere to help me." I look around the sea of faces, all wearing the same look. "Oh," I say.

I sit up as the details of that night flood my brain. The rush of footsteps in the dark. The guy shoving my pizza delivery bag at my face and grabbing me from behind, then pushing my face into a snowy bush. "He had a knife," I say. A shiver runs up my spine as I remember the click in my ear.

Everybody's silent for a second. And then Bridget says, "So there you go. You didn't start it. Next question?"

"So the guy . . ." I say, passing my hand over my eyes, trying to concentrate. It's like I can't quite put all the details together.

"The guy who saved you had a vision. He was waiting for you," Rowan says.

"Right," Trey says. "He saved you, and passed on the vision to you."

"And you passed it to me, and that guy probably got it from someone else, too," Sawyer says. "The point is, you didn't start it. You," he says, touching my shoulder, "are not responsible for this."

It's like somebody pulled a hundred-pound weight off my back. "I didn't start it," I whisper.

Rowan smiles. "You didn't start it."

"And," Trey says, "neither did Dad. You aren't heredi-tarily insane. Yet, anyway."

It's almost too much for me to take in.

I look at Bridget. "What the hell, Bridge," I say.

She shrugs, looking smug. "Logic," she says.

I think of all the risks we took. The crash. The school shooting. Nearly drowning. The graduation stampede. We all could have died so many times. And it wasn't my fault. It wasn't my responsibility. I can hardly comprehend it. All I know is that I feel true relief for the first time in over six months.

Later, when Trey and Ben take a walk in the school play-ground in the moonlight and Rowan goes inside to chat with Charlie, Sawyer and I drive Bridget Brinkerhoff back to her hotel. She's done getting treatments in Chicago for a while, and will travel back home to Michigan with her parents tomorrow—via land, of course. Maybe we'll see her again. Maybe we won't. That's how we leave it.

But when Sawyer and I drive back without her, it feels like a really long chapter of my life is over. There's just one thing missing. One thing I have to do before I can really close the door on this.

"Can we stop at that complex across from the Traverse Apartments for a minute?" I ask.

Sawyer glances sidelong at me. "You wanna have sexy time *there*?"

I laugh. "No." A wave of nerves washes over me. "I just want to go back to the scene of the crime. The incident."

"Where you got mugged?"

"Yeah."

He turns off to head in that direction, and soon he's pulling into the parking lot.

"There," I say, pointing to a parking spot.

He parks and we get out of the car. I walk to the sidewalk where I was standing when I heard the rush of footsteps. Walk up to the bush that had been full of snow. It's beautiful and green now, with a few extra-long spears sticking out of it.

"Where did the rescue guy come from?" Sawyer asks.

I tug on one of the spears. "I don't know. My face was full of snow. I didn't see. Somewhere over there." I look up and point. "I was so scared."

Sawyer pulls me close in a side hug and holds me.

"Do you want to knock on doors?" he asks, only partly teasing.

"Thinking about it," I say. "But what are the chances he actually lives here? The vision god isn't that thoughtful to make these tragedies convenient, you know?"

We stand for a few more minutes, Sawyer letting me take my time to process. And now I can't believe I never put the two incidents together. Like Bridget says, it's logic. I shake my head, deep in thought.

A door to one of the buildings opens.

Four twentysomething guys come out, talking a little too loudly for the time of night it is. Sawyer's grip on my shoulder grows noticeably tighter as the group heads toward us, but they are talking about going on a beer run and not paying attention to us.

"Hey," Sawyer says in greeting as they walk past.

They respond pleasantly. I relax a bit as they pile into a car nearby.

As the fourth guy opens the back door and puts his foot inside, he looks at us and nods once. The safety lighting from the building shines on him, and I see a raised scar down one cheek. With the door still open, his hand on the inside handle, ready to pull it shut, he pauses and looks at me. Hard.

Our eyes lock. I swallow and give a closed-lip smile.

He hesitates, and when the other guys start hollering for him to hurry up, a look of clarity washes over him. He smiles at me and nods. And I'm probably projecting, but it's almost like he's really pleased to see me. Alive.

My chest tightens.

The guy's fingers flit in an awkward wave as he sits down and closes the door.

The driver pulls out of his parking space and speeds off.

When they're gone, I look at Sawyer and he looks at me.

We shrug and grin together. "Do you think that was him?" Sawyer asks, incredulous.

"I don't know. I doubt it. Too much of a coincidence." I hesitate. "But maybe I'll just pretend it's him, and that we have an understanding now."

And then Sawyer plants a kiss on my lips, and we get in the car and go home.

Because it's over. For real this time.

All I know is that for a while there, we were invincible. And every now and then, when I see a news story about an ordinary hero saving people from an almost certain tragedy, I glance at Sawyer, and he glances at me, and we know the vision curse continues on without us. I think about the heroes and wonder how it happened for them—how they came to be saved, so that they, too, could rescue someone. I wonder about their stories and the people who have come in and touched their lives, and then disappeared again . . . or stayed in them.

But those are not my stories to tell.

About the Author

Lisa McMann is the author of the *New York Times* bestelling Wake trilogy, *Cryer's Cross*, *Dead to You*, the Visions series, and the middle-grade dystopian fantasy series The Unwanteds. She lives with her family in the Phoenix area. Read more about Lisa and find her blog through her website at LISAMcMANN.com or, better yet, find her on Facebook (facebook.com/mcmannfan) or follow her on Twitter (twitter.com/lisa_mcmann).